*The
Education
of
Little Tree*

The
EDUCATION
of
LITTLE TREE

Forrest Carter
Foreword by Rennard Strickland

University of New Mexico Press
Albuquerque

Library of Congress Cataloging-in-Publication Data

Carter, Forrest.
The education of Little Tree.

Reprint. Originally published: New York: Delacorte
Press, © 1976. With new foreword.
1. Carter, Forrest—Biography—Youth.
2. Novelists, American—20th century—Biography.
3. Cherokee Indians—Biography. I. Title.
[PS3553.A777Z464 1986]   813'.54   85-28956
ISBN 0-8263-0879-1 (pbk.)

University of New Mexico Press paperback edition reprinted 1986
by arrangement with Cherokees Carter Corp. and Eleanor Friede, Inc.
Fifteenth paperbound 1993

Sharing Little Tree

Gramma said when you come on something good, first thing to do is share it with whoever you can find; that way, the good spreads out where no telling it will go. Which is right.

IN REISSUING Forrest Carter's *The Education of Little Tree*, the University of New Mexico Press is doing exactly what Gramma advised young Little Tree. The Press is sharing an important book. *Little Tree* is one of those rare books like *Huck Finn* that each new generation needs to discover and which needs to be read and reread regularly. *The Education of Little Tree* is a fine and sustaining book, wonderfully funny and deeply poignant.

Little Tree's author, Forrest Carter, wrote a number of important books including the popular *Outlaw Josey Wales;* he wrote one great book, *The Education of Little Tree*. Originally to have been called "Me and Grandpa," *Little Tree* is Carter's autobiographical remembrances of life with his Eastern Cherokee Hill country grandparents. But *Little Tree* is more, much more than a touching account of 1930s depression-era life. This book is a human document of universal meaning. *The Education of Little Tree* speaks to the human spirit and reaches the very depth of the human soul.

Everyone who has ever read *The Education of Little Tree*

seems to remember when and where and how they came to know the book. Whether they saw it in the autobiography section of a chain bookseller; or heard it reviewed as "Book of the Week" on a television book show; or found it on the gift table at a tribal souvenir shop while passing through an Indian reservation, *Little Tree's* readers passionately remember these first meetings. For *The Education of Little Tree* is a book from which one never quite recovers. After reading *Little Tree* one never again sees the world in quite the same way.

Upon publication in 1977 *The Education of Little Tree* was widely reviewed and universally acclaimed. Reviewers as diverse as those of *The New York Times* and local mountain weeklies saw in *The Education of Little Tree* an inspirational, autobiographical remembrance of a young Indian boy which might provide a fresh perspective for a mechanistic and materialistic modern world. Thus *Little Tree* found its first and most loyal readership among those who cared about the young, about "growing up," about the Indian, about the earth, and about the relationship of man and the earth.

Soon *Little Tree* began to find fans among other groups. Teenagers took to the book almost as a cult. The values as well as the prose touched many who didn't usually read. Younger children found *Little Tree* on their own. Librarians began to find *Little Tree* missing from the shelves. Students of Native American life discovered the book to be as accurate as it was mystical and romantic. Elementary-school teachers learned that *Little Tree* fascinated their seemingly world-weary charges. But most generally the love of *Little Tree* passed from reader to reader with the increasingly hard-to-find borrowed copy of the book.

With this University of New Mexico Press edition, *The Education of Little Tree* is again available. Old and new readers can once more share this incredibly touching and deeply moving story which informs the heart and educates the spirit.

Rennard Strickland
November 1985

Contents

CONTENTS

For The Cherokee

The
Education
of
Little Tree

Little Tree

MA LASTED a year after Pa was gone. That's how I came to live with Granpa and Granma when I was five years old.

The kinfolks had raised some mortal fuss about it, according to Granma, after the funeral.

There in the gullied backyard of our hillside shack, they had stood around in a group and thrashed it out proper as to where I was to go, while they divided up the painted bedstead and the table and chairs.

Granpa had not said anything. He stood back at the edge of the yard, on the fringe of the crowd, and Granma stood behind him. Granpa was half Cherokee and Granma full blood.

He stood above the rest of the folks; tall, six-foot-four with his big, black hat and shiny, black suit that was only worn to church and funerals. Granma had kept her eyes to the ground, but Granpa had looked at me, over the crowd, and so I had edged to him across the yard and held onto his leg and wouldn't turn loose even when they tried to take me away.

Granma said I didn't holler one bit, nor cry, just held on; and after a long time, them tugging and me holding,

Granpa had reached down and placed his big hand on my head.

"Leave him be," he had said. And so they left me be. Granpa seldom spoke in a crowd, but when he did, Granma said, folks listened.

We walked down the hillside in the dark winter afternoon and onto the road that led into town. Granpa led the way down the side of the road, my clothes slung over his shoulder in a tow sack. I learned right off that when you walked behind Granpa, you trotted; and Granma, behind me, occasionally lifted her skirts to keep up.

When we reached the sidewalks in town, we walked the same way, Granpa leading, until we came to the back of the bus station. We stood there for a long time; Granma reading the lettering on the front of the buses as they came and went. Granpa said that Granma could read fancy as anybody. She picked out our bus, right on the nose, just as dusk dark was settin' in.

We waited until all the people were on the bus, and it was a good thing, because trouble set up the minute we set foot inside the door. Granpa led the way, me in the middle and Granma was standing on the lower step, just inside the door. Granpa pulled his snap-purse from his forward pants pocket and stood ready to pay.

"Where's your tickets?" the bus driver said real loud, and everybody in the bus set up to take notice of us. This didn't bother Granpa one bit. He told the bus driver we stood ready to pay, and Granma whispered from behind me for Granpa to tell where we were going. Granpa told him.

The bus driver told Granpa how much it was and while Granpa counted out the money real careful—for the light wasn't good to count by—the bus driver turned around to the crowd in the bus and lifted his right hand and said, "*How!*" and laughed, and all the people laughed. I felt better about it, knowing they was friendly and didn't take offense because we didn't have a ticket.

Then we walked to the back of the bus, and I noticed a sick lady. She was unnatural black all around her eyes and her mouth was red all over from blood; but as we passed, she put a hand over her mouth and took it off and hollered real loud, "Wa . . . hooo!" But I figured the pain must have passed right quick, because she laughed, and everybody else laughed. The man sitting beside her was laughing too and he slapped his leg. He had a big shiny pin on his tie, so I knew they was rich and could get a doctor if they needed one.

I sat in the middle between Granma and Granpa, and Granma reached across and patted Granpa on the hand, and he held her hand across my lap. It felt good, and so I slept.

It was deep into the night when we got off the bus on the side of a gravel road. Granpa set off walking, me and Granma behind. It was cracking cold. The moon was out, like half of a fat watermelon, and silvering the road ahead until it curved out of sight.

It wasn't until we turned off the road, onto wagon ruts with grass in the middle, that I noticed the mountains. Dark and shadowed, they were, with the half-moon right atop a ridge that lifted so high it bent your head back to look. I shivered at the blackness of the mountains.

Granma spoke from behind me, "Wales, he's tiring out." Granpa stopped and turned. He looked down at me and the big hat shadowed his face.

"It's better to wear out when ye've lost something," he said. He turned and set off again, but now it was easier to keep up. Granpa had slowed down, so I figured he was tired too.

After a long time, we turned off the wagon ruts onto a foot trail and headed dead set into the mountains. Seemed like we'd come straight up against a mountain, but as we walked, the mountains seemed to open up and fold in around us on all sides.

The sounds of our walking began to echo, and stirrings

came from around us, and whispers and sighs began to feather through the trees like everything had come alive. And it was warm. There was a tinkle and a bobble and swishing beside us, a mountain branch rolling over rocks and making pools where it paused and rushed on again. We were into the hollows of the mountains.

The half-moon dropped out of sight behind the ridge and spewed silver light over the sky. It gave the hollow a gray-light dome that reflected down on us.

Granma began to hum a tune behind me and I knew it was Indian, and needed no words for its meaning to be clear, and it made me feel safe.

A hound bayed so sudden, I jumped. Long and mourning, breaking into sobs that the echoes picked up and carried farther and farther away, back into the mountains.

Granpa chuckled, "That'd be ol' Maud—ain't got the smell sense of a lap dog—dependent on her ears."

In a minute, we were covered up with hounds, whining around Granpa and sniffing at me to get the new scent. Ol' Maud bayed again, right close this time, and Granpa said, "Shet up, Maud!" And then she knew who it was and she came running and leaping on us.

We crossed a foot log over the spring branch and there was the cabin, logged and set back under big trees with the mountain at its back and a porch running clear across the front.

The cabin had a wide hall separating the rooms. The hall was open on both ends. Some people call it a "gallery," but mountain folks call it a "dogtrot," because the hounds trotted through there. On one side was a big room for cooking, eating and settin', and across the dogtrot on the other side were two bedrooms. One was Granpa and Granma's. The other was to be mine.

I laid out on the springy softness of deer hide webbing, stretched in the frame of hickory posts. Through the open window, I could see the trees across the spring branch, dark in the ghost light. The thought of Ma came rushing on me and the strangeness of where I was.

A hand brushed my head. It was Granma sitting beside me, on the floor; her full skirts around her, the plaited hair streaked with silver falling forward of her shoulders and into her lap. She watched out the window too, and low and soft she began to sing:

"They now have sensed him coming
  The forest and the wood-wind
Father mountain makes him welcome with his song.
  They have no fear of Little Tree
  They know his heart is kindness
And they sing, 'Little tree is not alone.'

Even silly little Lay-nah
  With her babbling, talking waters
Is dancing through the mountains with her cheer
  'Oh listen to my singing,
  Of a brother come amongst us
Little Tree is our brother, and Little Tree is here.'

Awi usdi the little deer
  And Min-e-lee the quail-hen
Even Kagu the crow takes up the song
  'Brave is the heart of Little Tree
  And kindness is his strength
And Little Tree will never be alone.'"

Granma sang and rocked slowly back and forth. And I could hear the wind talking, and Lay-nah, the spring branch, singing about me and telling all my brothers.

I knew I was Little Tree, and I was happy that they loved me and wanted me. And so I slept, and I did not cry.

The Way

IT HAD TAKEN Granma, sitting in the rocker that creaked with her slight weight as she worked and hummed, while the pine knots spluttered in the fireplace, a week of evenings to make the boot moccasins. With a hook knife, she had cut the deer leather and made the strips that she wove around the edges. When she had finished, she soaked the moccasins in water and I put them on wet and walked them dry, back and forth across the floor, until they fitted soft and giving, light as air.

This morning I slipped the moccasins on last, after I had jumped into my overalls and buttoned my jacket. It was dark and cold—too early even for the morning whisper wind to stir the trees.

Granpa had said I could go with him on the high trail, if I got up, and he had said he would not wake me.

"A man rises of his own will in the morning," he had spoken down to me and he did not smile. But Granpa had made many noises in his rising, bumping the wall of my room and talking uncommonly loud to Granma, and so I had heard, and I was first out, waiting with the hounds in the darkness.

"So. Ye're here," Granpa sounded surprised.

"Yes, sir," I said, and kept the proud out of my voice.

Granpa pointed his finger at the hounds jumping and prancing around us. "Ye'll stay," he ordered, and they tucked in their tails and whined and begged and ol' Maud set up a howl. But they didn't follow us. They stood, all together in a hopeless little bunch, and watched us leave the clearing.

I had been up the low trail that followed the bank of the spring branch, twisting and turning with the hollow until it broke out into a meadow where Granpa had his barn and kept his mule and cow. But this was the high trail that forked off to the right and took to the side of the mountain, sloping always upward as it traveled along the hollow. I trotted behind Granpa and I could feel the upward slant of the trail.

I could feel something more, as Granma said I would. Mon-o-lah, the earth mother, came to me through my moccasins. I could feel her push and swell here, and sway and give there . . . and the roots that veined her body and the life of the water-blood, deep inside her. She was warm and springy and bounced me on her breast, as Granma said she would.

The cold air steamed my breath in clouds and the spring branch fell far below us. Bare tree branches dripped water from ice prongs that teethed their sides, and as we walked higher there was ice on the trail. Gray light eased the darkness away.

Granpa stopped and pointed by the side of the trail. "There she is—turkey run—see?" I dropped to my hands and knees and saw the tracks: little sticklike impressions coming out from a center hub.

"Now," Granpa said, "we'll fix the trap." And he moved off the trail until he found a stump hole.

We cleaned it out, first the leaves, and then Granpa pulled out his long knife and cut into the spongy ground and we scooped up the dirt, scattering it among the leaves.

When the hole was deep, so that I couldn't see over the rim, Granpa pulled me out and we dragged tree branches to cover it and, over these, spread armfuls of leaves. Then, with his long knife, Granpa dug a trail sloping downward into the hole and back toward the turkey run. He took the grains of red Indian corn from his pocket and scattered them down the trail, and threw a handful into the hole.

"Now we will go," he said, and set off again up the high trail. Ice, spewed from the earth like frosting, crackled under our feet. The mountain opposite us moved closer as the hollow far below became a narrow slit, showing the spring branch like the edge of a steel knife, sunk in the bottom of its cleavage.

We sat down in the leaves, off the trail, just as the first sun touched the top of the mountain across the hollow. From his pocket, Granpa pulled out a sour biscuit and deer meat for me, and we watched the mountain while we ate.

The sun hit the top like an explosion, sending showers of glitter and sparkle into the air. The sparkling of the icy trees hurt the eyes to look, and it moved down the mountain like a wave as the sun backed the night shadow down and down. A crow scout sent three hard calls through the air, warning we were there.

And now the mountain popped and gave breathing sighs that sent little puffs of steam into the air. She pinged and murmured as the sun released the trees from their death armor of ice.

Granpa watched, same as me, and listened as the sounds grew with the morning wind that set up a low whistle in the trees.

"She's coming alive," he said, soft and low, without taking his eyes from the mountain.

"Yes, sir," I said, "she's coming alive." And I knew right then that me and Granpa had us an understanding that most folks didn't know.

The night shadow backed down and across a little meadow, heavy with grass and shining in the sun bath. The meadow was set into the side of the mountain. Granpa pointed. There was quail fluttering and jumping in the grass, feeding on the seeds. Then he pointed up toward the icy blue sky.

There were no clouds but at first I didn't see the speck that came over the rim. It grew larger. Facing into the sun, so that the shadow did not go before him, the bird sped down the side of the mountain; a skier on the tree-tops, wings half-folded . . . like a brown bullet . . . faster and faster, toward the quail.

Granpa chuckled. "It's ol' Tal-con, the hawk."

The quail rose in a rush and sped into the trees—but one was slow. The hawk hit. Feathers flew into the air and then the birds were on the ground; the hawk's head rising and falling with the death blows. In a moment he rose with the dead quail clutched in his claws, back up the side of the mountain and over the rim.

I didn't cry, but I know I looked sad, because Granpa said, "Don't feel sad, Little Tree. It is The Way. Tal-con caught the slow and so the slow will raise no children who are also slow. Tal-con eats a thousand ground rats who eat the eggs of the quail—both the quick and the slow eggs—and so Tal-con lives by The Way. He helps the quail."

Granpa dug a sweet root from the ground with his knife and peeled it so that it dripped with its juicy winter cache of life. He cut it in half and handed me the heavy end.

"It is The Way," he said softly. "Take only what ye need. When ye take the deer, do not take the best. Take the smaller and the slower and then the deer will grow stronger and always give you meat. Pa-koh, the panther, knows and so must ye."

And he laughed, "Only Ti-bi, the bee, stores more than

he can use . . . and so he is robbed by the bear, and the
'coon . . . and the Cherokee. It is so with people who store
and fat themselves with more than their share. They will
have it taken from them. And there will be wars over it . . .
and they will make long talks, trying to hold more than
their share. They will say a flag stands for their right to
do this . . . and men will die because of the words and the
flag . . . but they will not change the rules of The Way."

We went back down the trail, and the sun was high over
us when we reached the turkey trap. We could hear them
before we saw the trap. They were in there, gobbling and
making loud whistles of alarm.

"Ain't no closing over the door, Granpa," I said. "Why
don't they just lower their heads and come out?"

Granpa stretched full length into the hole and pulled
out a big squawking turkey, tied his legs with a throng and
grinned up at me.

"Ol' Tel-qui is like some people. Since he knows everything, he won't never look down to see what's around him.
Got his head stuck up in the air too high to learn anything."

"Like the bus driver" I asked. I couldn't forget the bus
driver fussing at Granpa.

"The bus driver?" Granpa looked puzzled, then he
laughed, and kept laughing while he stuck his head back
in the hole, pulling out another turkey.

"I reckin," he chuckled, "like the bus driver. He did
kind of gobble now, come to think of it. But that's a
burden fer him to tote around, Little Tree. Nothing fer
us to burden our heads about."

Granpa laid them out on the ground, legs tied. There
were six of them, and now he pointed down at them.
"They're all about the same age . . . ye can tell by the
thickness of the combs. We only need three so now ye
choose, Little Tree."

I walked around them, flopping on the ground. I

squatted and studied them, and walked around them again. I had to be careful. I got down on my hands and knees and crawled among them, until I had pulled out the three smallest I could find.

Granpa said nothing. He pulled the throngs from the legs of the others and they took to wing, beating down the side of the mountain. He slung two of the turkeys over his shoulder.

"Can ye carry the other?" he asked.

"Yes, sir," I said, not sure that I had done right. A slow grin broke Granpa's bony face. "If ye was not Little Tree ... I would call ye Little Hawk."

I followed Granpa down the trail. The turkey was heavy, but it felt good over my shoulder. The sun had tilted toward the farther mountain and drifted through the branches of the trees beside the trail, making burnt gold patterns where we walked. The wind had died in that late afternoon of winter, and I heard Granpa, ahead of me, humming a tune. I would have liked to live that time forever ... for I knew I had pleased Granpa. I had learned The Way.

Trailing through the mountains in the winter's evening sun
Walking through the patterns on the trail
Sloping towards the cabin; been on the turkey run
It's a heaven that the Cherokee knows well.

Watch along the mountain rim and see the morning birth
Listen for the wind song through the tree
Feel the life a'springing from Mon-o-lah, the earth
And you'll know The Way of all the Cherokee.

Know the death in life is here with every breaking day
That one without the other, cannot be
Learn the wisdom of Mon-o-lah,
        and then you'll know The Way
And touch the soul of all the Cherokee.

Shadows on a Cabin Wall

IN THE EVENINGS of that winter, we sat in front of the stone fireplace. Lighter knots, taken from the centers of rotted stumps, sputtered and flickered from the thick, red resin, throwing on the wall shadows that jumped and contracted, only to leap up again, making the walls come alive with fantastic etchings appearing and disappearing, growing and receding. There were long silences while we watched the flames and the dancing shadows. Then Granpa would break the silence with some of his comments on the "readings."

Twice a week, every Saturday and Sunday nights, Granma lit the coal oil lamp and read to us. Lighting the lamp was a luxury, and I'm sure it was done on account of me. We had to be careful of the coal oil. Once a month, me and Granpa walked to the settlement, and I carried the coal oil can with a root stuck in its snout, so that not a drop was spilled on the way back. It cost a nickel to fill it, and Granpa showed a lot of trust in me, letting me carry it all the way back to the cabin.

When we went, we always carried a list of books made out by Granma, and Granpa presented the list to the librarian, and turned in the books that Granma had sent back. She didn't know the names of modern authors, I don't suppose, because the list always had the name of Mr. Shakespeare (anything we hadn't read by him, for she didn't know the titles). Sometimes this caused Granpa a lot of trouble with the librarian. She would go and pull out different stories by Mr. Shakespeare and read the titles. If Granpa still couldn't remember by the title, she would have to read a page—sometimes Granpa would tell her to keep reading, and she would read several pages. Sometimes I would recognize the story before Granpa, and I would pull on his pants leg and nod at him that we had read that one, but it got to where it was kind of a contest—Granpa trying to say before I recognized it, and then changing his mind, and this got the librarian all confused.

She fretted some at first, and asked Granpa what he wanted with books if he couldn't *read*, and Granpa explained that Granma read us the books. After that she kept her own list of what we had read. She was nice and smiled when we came in the door. Once she gave me a stick of red striped candy which I saved until we were outside. I broke it in two and split with Granpa. He would only take the little piece, as I didn't break it exactly even.

We kept the dictionary checked out all the time, as I had to learn five words a week, starting at the front, which caused me considerable trouble, since I had to try to make up sentences in my talk through the week using the words. This is hard, when all the words you learn for the week start with A, or B if you're into the B's.

But there were other books; one was *The Decline and Fall of the Roman Empire* . . . and there were authors like Shelley and Byron that Granma hadn't known about, but the librarian sent them along.

Granma read slowly, bending her head to the book with her long hair plaits trailing to the floor. Granpa rocked with a slow creak, back and forth, and when we got to an exciting place, I always knew, because Granpa stopped rocking.

When Granma read about Macbeth, I could see the castle and the witches taking shape in the shadows, alive on the cabin walls, and I'd edge closer to Granpa's rocker. He'd stop rocking when Granma got to the stabbings and the blood and all. Granpa said none of it would come about if Lady Macbeth had minded doing what a woman was supposed to do and kept her nose out of the business that rightly ought to have been done by Mr. Macbeth, and besides, she wasn't much of a lady, and he couldn't figure out why she was called such, anyhow. Granpa said all this in the heat of the first reading. Later on, after he had mulled it over in his mind, he commented that something was undoubtedly wrong with the woman (he refused to call her Lady). He said, however, he had seen a doe deer one time, that was in heat and couldn't find a buck, go slap-dab mad, running into trees and finally drowning herself in the creek. He said there was no way of knowing, because Mr. Shakespeare didn't indicate as such, but it all could be laid at the door of Mr. Macbeth—and indications was along that line—as the man seemed to have trouble doing just about anything.

He worried about it considerable, but finally settled on laying the biggest part of the fault on Mrs. Macbeth, because she could have taken out her heat-meanness in other ways, such as buttin' her head agin' a wall, if nothing else, instead of killing folks.

Granpa taken the side of Julius Caesar in his killing. He said he couldn't put his stamp on everything Mr. Caesar done—and, in fact, had no way of knowing all he had done—but he said that was the low-downest bunch he'd ever heard of, Brutus and all the others, the way they went slipping up on a feller, outnumbering him and stabbing him to death. He said if they had a difference with Mr. Caesar, they'd ought to made theirselves known and settled it square out. He got so het up about it that Granma had to quiet him down. She said we was, all present, in support of Mr. Caesar at his killing, so there wasn't anybody for him to argue with, and anyhow, it happened so long ago, she doubted if anything could be done about it now.

But where we run into real trouble was over George Washington. To understand what it meant to Granpa, you have to know something of the background.

Granpa had all the natural enemies of a mountain man. Add on to that he was poor without saying and more Indian than not. I suppose today, the enemies would be called "the establishment," but to Granpa, whether sheriff, state or federal revenue agent, or politician of any stripe, he called them "the law," meaning powerful monsters who had no regard for how folks had to live and get by.

Granpa said he was a "man, full-growed and standing before he knowed it was agin' the law to make whiskey." He said he had a cousin who never did know, and went to his grave-mound not knowing. He said his cousin always suspicioned that the law had it in for him because he didn't vote "right"; but he never could figure exactly which was the right way to vote. Granpa always believed that his cousin fretted himself into an early grave, worrying at voting time which was the way to vote, in order to clear up his "trouble." He got so nervous about it, he taken to heavy drinking spells, which eventually killed him. Granpa laid his death at the door of the politicians, who, he said, were responsible for just about all the killings in history if you could check up on it.

In reading the old history book in later years, I discovered that Granma had skipped the chapters about George Washington fighting the Indians, and I know that she had read only the good about George Washington to give Granpa someone to look to and admire. He had no regard whatsoever for Andrew Jackson and, as I say, nobody else in politics that I can call to mind.

After listening to Granma's readings, Granpa began to refer to George Washington in many of his comments . . . holding him out as the big hope that there *could* be a good man in politics.

Until Granma slipped up and read about the whiskey tax.

She read where George Washington was going to put a tax on whiskey-makers and decide who could make whiskey and who couldn't. She read where Mr. Thomas Jefferson told George Washington that it was the wrong thing to do; that poor mountain farmers didn't have nothing but little hillside patches, and couldn't raise much corn like the big landowners in the flatlands did. She read where Mr. Jefferson warned that the only way the mountain folk had of realizing a profit from their corn was to make it into whiskey, and that it had caused trouble in Ireland and Scotland (as a matter of fact that's where Scotch whiskey got its burnt taste—from fellers having to run from the King's men and leaving their pots to scorch). But George Washington wouldn't listen, and he put on the whiskey tax.

It hit Granpa deep. He stopped his rocker but he didn't say anything, just stared into the fire with a lost look in his eyes. Granma felt sorry about it for after the reading she patted Granpa on his shoulder and slipped her arm around his waist as they went off to bed. I felt might near as bad about it as Granpa.

It was a month later, when me and Granpa was on the way to the settlement that I realized how he had been taken under. We had walked down the trail, Granpa leading, onto the wagon ruts . . . and then alongside the road. Every once in a while a car passed us but Granpa never looked around for he never accepted a ride. But of a sudden, a car pulled up beside us. It was an open car, without windows, and had a canvas top on it. The man inside was dressed up like a politician and I knew Granpa wouldn't ride, but I got a surprise.

The feller leaned over and hollered above the chugging sound, "Want a ride?"

Granpa stood for just a minute, then said, "Thankee," and got in, motioning for me to get in the back. Down the road we went, and it was exciting to me at how fast we covered ground.

Now Granpa always stood and sat straight as an arrow, but sitting in the car with his hat on, he was too tall. He refused to slouch, so he was forced to bend, back straight, toward the windshield. This gave him the appearance of studying the driving of the politician at the wheel, as well as the road ahead. It made the politician nervous, I could tell, but Granpa didn't pay him any mind whatsoever. Finally, the politician said, "Going into town?"

Granpa said, "Yep." We rode along some more.

"Are you a farmer?"

"Some," Granpa said.

"I'm a professor at the State Teachers College," the professor said, and I thought he sounded right uppity about it, though I was surprised and pleased that he wasn't a politician. Granpa didn't say anything.

"Are you Indian?" the professor asked.

"Yep," Granpa said.

"Oh," said the professor, like that explained me and Granpa entirely.

Of a sudden, Granpa whirled his head toward the professor and said, "What do you know about George Washington puttin' on the whiskey tax?" You would of thought that Granpa had reached over and slapped the professor.

"The whiskey tax?" he shouted, real loud.

"Yep," Granpa said, "the whiskey tax."

The professor looked red and nervous of a sudden, and it dawned on me that he might have had something personal to do with puttin' the whiskey tax on himself.

"I don't know," he said. "Do you mean the General George Washington?"

"Was they more than one?" Granpa asked him, surprised. It surprised me too.

"Noooo," the professor said, "but I don't know anything about it." Which sounded kind of suspicious to me, and I could see it didn't set well with Granpa either. The professor looked straight ahead, and it seemed to me we was going faster and faster. Granpa was studying the road ahead through the windshield, and I knew right then why we had taken the ride.

Granpa spoke again, but his tone didn't hold much hope, "Do ye know if General Washington ever got a lick on the head—I mean in all them battles maybe a rifle ball hit him on the side of the head?" The professor didn't look at Granpa and was acting more nervous all the time.

"I, that is," he stuttered, "I teach English and I don't know *anything* about George Washington."

We reached the edge of the settlement and Granpa said we would get out. We wasn't anywheres near into where we was going. When we got out on the side of the road, Granpa taken off his hat to thank the professor, but he didn't hardly wait for us to hit the ground before he spun off in a cloud of dust. Granpa said it was about the kind of manners he expected from folks like that. He agreed that the professor acted suspicious, and that he could have been a politician making out to be a professor. He said lots of politicians moved around amongst honest people claiming they wasn't politicians. But, Granpa said, you couldn't discount him being a professor, for he had heard that more of them was crazy than not.

Granpa said he figured George Washington took a lick on the head some way or other in all his fighting, which accounted for an action like the whiskey tax. He said he had an uncle once that was kicked in the head by a mule and never was quite right after that; though he said he had his private opinion (never stated public) that his uncle used that on occasion; like the time a feller come home to his cabin and caught his uncle in bed with the feller's wife. He said his uncle run out in the yard on all fours, hunkered down like a hog and commenced to eat dirt. But, he said, nobody could tell whether he was puttin' it on or not . . .

leastwise, the feller couldn't. Granpa said his uncle lived to a ripe age and died peaceable in his bedstead. Anyway, he said it wasn't for him to judge. The condition of George Washington sounded reasonable to me and could of accounted for some of his other troubles.

Fox and Hounds

IT WAS LATE of a winter afternoon when Granpa took ol' Maud and Ringer into the cabin because he said he didn't want them embarrassed before the other hounds. I figured something was to happen. Granma already knew. Her eyes were twinkling like black lights and she put a deer shirt on me, just like Granpa's, and placed her hand on my shoulder like she done him, and I felt might near growed-up.

I didn't ask, but I hung around. Granma gave me a sack with biscuits and meat and said, "I'll sit on the porch tonight and listen; and I will hear you."

We went into the yard and Granpa whistled up the dogs and off we set, up the hollow by the spring branch. The hounds ran back and forth, hurrying us up.

Granpa kept his hounds for only two reasons. One was his corn patch where every spring and summer, he assigned ol' Maud and Ringer to stay and guard against deer, 'coon, hogs and crow getting all his corn.

Like Granpa said, ol' Maud had no smell sense atall and was practical worthless on a fox trail; but she had keen hearing and eyesight, and this gave her something she could do and take pride in knowing she was of worth. Granpa said if a hound or anybody else has got no feeling of worth, then it's a bad thing.

Ringer had been a good trail dog. He was getting old now. His tail was broke, which made him look disheartened, and he couldn't see nor hear very well. Granpa said he put Ringer with ol' Maud so he could help and feel that he was of worth in his old age; that it sort of dignified him, which it did for Ringer walked around right stiff-legged and dignified, especially during the periods when he was working at the corn patch.

Granpa fed ol' Maud and Ringer at the barn up in the hollow during corn raising time, for this wasn't far from the corn patch. They stayed there faithful. Ol' Maud was Ringer's eyes and ears. She would see something in the corn patch and take off after it, raising howls like she owned that corn patch, and Ringer would follow, doing the same.

They'd go crashing through the corn; and maybe ol' Maud would run right past a 'coon if she didn't see it, for she sure couldn't smell it . . . but Ringer, following behind her, could. He'd put his nose to the ground and go braying after that 'coon. He'd run that 'coon out of the patch and hold onto his trail by smell until he run into a tree. Then he'd come back kind of sad; but him and ol' Maud never give up. They done their job.

The other reason Granpa kept hounds was for pure fun, trailing fox. He never used dogs to hunt game. He didn't need them. Granpa knew the watering and feeding places, the habit and trails, even the thinking and character of all the game, far better than any hound could learn.

The red fox runs in a circle when he is chased by hounds. With his den in the center, he will start on a circle swing that measures maybe a mile, sometimes more, across the middle. All the time he's running, he'll use tricks: backtracking, running in water and laying false trails; but he'll stick to the circle. As he grows tired, he will make the circle smaller and smaller, until he retreats to his den. He "dens up," they call it.

The more he runs, the hotter he gets, and his mouth sweats out stronger smells that the dogs pick up on the trail, and so get louder with their baying. It is called a "hot trail."

When the gray fox runs, he runs in a figure 8, and his den is just about where he crosses his trail each time to make the 8

Granpa knew the thinking of the 'coon too and laughed at his mischievous ways, and swore a solemn oath that on occasion, the 'coon had laughed at him. He knew where the turkey ran, and could track a bee from water to hive with a look of his eye. He could make the deer come to him, because he knew his curious nature; and he could ease through a covey of quail without stirring a wing. But he never bothered them, except for what he needed and I *know* they understood.

Granpa lived *with* the game, not *at* it. The white mountain men were a hardy lot and Granpa bore with them well. But they would take their dogs and clatter all over the mountains chasing game this way and that, until everything run for cover. If they saw a dozen turkey, why they killed a dozen turkey, if they could.

But they respected Granpa as a master woodsman. I could see it in their eyes and the touching of their hat brims when they met him at the crossroads store. They stayed out of Granpa's hollows and mountains with their guns and dogs, whilst they complained a lot about the game getting scarcer and scarcer where they was. Granpa often shook his head at their comments and never said anything. But he told me. They would never understand The Way of the Cherokee.

With the dogs loping behind, I trotted close behind

Granpa, because it was that mysterious, exciting time in the hollows when the sun had sunk and the light faded from red to shady blood, and kept changing and darkening, as if the daylight was alive but dying. Even the dusk breeze was sly with a whisper as if it had things to tell that it couldn't say out open.

The game was going to its beds and the night creatures was coming out for the hunt. As we passed the meadow by the barn, Granpa stopped and I stood practical under him.

An owl was flying toward us down the hollow, moving in the air no higher than Granpa's head; and passed right by, making no sound, not a whisper nor whir of wing and settled silent as a ghost in the barn.

"Screech owl," Granpa said, "the one ye hear sometimes at night that sounds like a woman paining. Going to catch some rats." I sure didn't want to disturb that ol' owl and rat catching, and kept Granpa between me and the barn as we passed.

Dark fell in close, and the mountains moved in on either side as we walked. Before long, we came to a Y in the trail, and Granpa taken the left. Now there was no more room for the trail except right on the edge of the spring branch. Granpa called this the "Narrows." Seemed like you could stretch out your arms on either side and touch the mountains. Straight up they went, dark and feathered with treetops, and left a thin slice of stars above us.

Way off, a mourning dove called, long and throaty, and the mountains picked it up and echoed the sound over and over, carrying it farther and farther away until you wondered how many mountains and hollows that call would travel—and it died away, so far, it was more like a memory than a sound.

It was lonesome, and I trotted right up on Granpa's heels. None of the hounds stayed behind me, which I wished they would. They stayed ahead of Granpa, running back to him now and then, whining and wanting him to send them off trailing.

The Narrows sloped upward, and before long I could hear big water running. It was a creek that crossed what Granpa called "Hangin' Gap."

We moved off the trail, up into the mountain above the creek. Granpa sent the dogs off. All he had to do was point and say, "Go!" and off they went, giving little yelps, like young'uns going berry picking Granpa said.

We sat down in a pine thicket above the creek. It was warm. Pine thickets give off heat, but if it's summertime, you want to sit amongst oak or hickory or some such, because pine gets plumb hot.

The stars were watering and moving around in the creek, riding on ripples and splashes. Granpa said we could commence to listen for the hounds in a little while, when they picked up ol' Slick's trail. That's what he called the fox.

Granpa said we was in ol' Slick's territory. He said he had knowed him about five years. Most people think that all fox hunters kill foxes, but it's not true. Granpa never killed a fox in his life. The reason for fox hunting is the hounds—to listen to their trailing. Granpa always called off the hounds when the fox denned up.

Granpa said that when things had got monotonous for ol' Slick he had gone so far as to come and set in the edge of the cabin clearing, trying to get Granpa and the hounds to trail him. It sometimes caused Granpa all manner of trouble with the hounds, as they yelped and bayed, with ol' Slick leading them up the hollow.

Granpa said he liked to slip up on ol' Slick when he was cantankerous and not in the mood for trailing. When a fox wants to den up, he will use ingenious tricks to throw off the hounds. When he is playful, he will play all over the countryside. He said the best part was that ol' Slick would *know* he was being paid back for sashaying around the cabin and troubling Granpa.

Sure enough, the moon broke over the mountain, a quarter used up. It sprinkled patterns through the pines and splashed lights off the creek, and made thin silver boats of the fog tearings sailing slow through the Narrows.

Granpa leaned back against a pine and spraddled out his legs. I done the same thing, and put the vittle sack right by me as it was my responsibility. Not far off a big bay sounded, long and hollow.

"That's ol' Rippitt," Granpa said, and laughed low, "and it's a damn lie. Rippitt knows what's wanted . . . but he can't wait, so he makes out like he's hit a trail-scent. Listen to how falsified his bay sounds. He knows he's a'lying." Sure enough, it *did* sound that-a-way.

"He's damn shore lying," I said. Me and Granpa could cuss when we wasn't around Granma.

In a minute the other hounds let him know, as they howled around him, not baying. In the mountains they call such a "bluffer dog." There was silence again.

In a little while a deep bay broke the stillness. It was long and far off, and I knew right then it was the real thing, because it carried excitement in it. The other hounds took it up.

"That was Blue Boy," Granpa said, "up and comin' to have the best nose in the mountains; and that's Little Red right behind him . . . and there's Bess." Another bay chimed in, this one kind of frantic. Granpa said, "And there's ol' Rippitt, gittin' in on the last."

They was in full voice now, moving farther and farther away; their chorus echoing backward and forward until it sounded like hounds all around. Then the sound disappeared.

"They're on the backside of Clinch Mountain," Granpa said. I listened hard, but I couldn't hear anything.

A nighthawk went "SEEeeeeeee!" from the side of the

mountain behind us, cutting the air with a sharp whistle. Across the creek, a hoot owl answered him, "WHO . . . WHO . . . WHOAREYouuuuu!"

Granpa laughed low. "Owl stays in the hollow, hawk stays on the ridges. Sometimes ol' hawk figures there's easy pickins around the water and ol' owl don't like it."

A fish flopped a splash in the creek. I was beginning to get worried. "Reckin," I whispered to Granpa, "that them hounds is *lost?*"

"Nope," Granpa said, "we'll hear 'em in a minute, and they'll come out on t'other side of Clinch Mountain and run across that ridge in front of us."

Sure enough they did. First they sounded far-off, then louder and louder; and they came, baying and yelping, longways along the ridge facing us and crossed the creek somewhere down below. Then they came along the side of the mountain behind us and set off again for Clinch Mountain. This time they ran on the near side of Clinch Mountain and we heard them all the way across it.

"Ol' Slick is tightening up the circle," Granpa said, "this time, after they cross the creek, ol' Slick may lead 'em right in front of us." Granpa was right. We heard them splashing across the creek not far below us . . . and while they was splashing and baying Granpa set up straight and grabbed my arm.

"There he is," Granpa whispered. And there he was. Coming along through willow poles on the creek bank, it was ol' Slick. He was trotting, with his tongue hanging out and a bushy tail dangling kind of careless behind him. He had pointed ears, and he jogged along real pickety, taking his time to go around a pile of brush. Once he stopped, lifted a front paw and licked it; then he turned his head back toward the baying of the hounds and came on.

Down in front of me and Granpa, there were some rocks that stuck up in the water, five or six of them that went out nearly to the middle of the creek. When ol' Slick reached where the rocks were, he stopped and looked back, like he was judging how far away the hounds was. Then he sat down, calm as you please with his back to us, and just sat there, looking at the creek. The moon glinted red off his coat, and the hounds was coming closer.

Granpa squeezed my arm. "Watch him now!" Ol' Slick jumped from the creek bank out onto the first rock. He stopped there a minute and danced on the rock. Then he jumped to the next one and danced again, then the next and the next until he reached the last one, nearly in the middle of the creek.

Then he came back, jumping from rock to rock, until he reached the one closest to the creek bank. He stopped and listened again; then stepped into the water and splashed up the creek, until he was out of sight. He sure cut the time close, because he had no more than disappeared when here come the hounds.

Blue Boy was leading with his nose right on the ground. Ol' Rippitt was crowding him, and Bess and Little Red was bunched right behind. Now and then, one of them would raise their nose and give out a "OOOWOOOOooooooooooh!" that tingled your blood.

They came to where the rocks went out into the creek and Blue Boy never hesitated; out he went, jumping from rock to rock, and the rest of them right behind.

When they reached the last rock in the middle of the creek, Blue Boy stopped but ol' Rippitt didn't. He jumped right in, like there wasn't no doubt about it, and started swimming for the other bank. Bess jumped in behind him and started swimming too.

Blue Boy raised his nose and commenced to sniff the air, and Little Red stayed there on the rock with him. In a minute here come Blue Boy and Little Red jumping back on the rocks toward us. They reached the bank, and Blue Boy led the way. Then he hit ol' Slick's trail and bayed long and loud, and Little Red chimed in.

Bess reversed herself while she was still swimming and come back, while ol' Rippitt was running up and down the other bank at a total loss. He was howling and yelping and running back and forth with his nose on the ground. When he heard Blue Boy, he hit the creek water in a dive and swam so hard he splashed water over his head until he made it to the bank and taken up the trail behind the rest of them.

Me and Granpa laughed so hard we nearly fell off the mountain. I did lose my foot-bracing hold on a pine sapling and rolled into cocklebur bushes. Granpa pulled me out and we was still laughing while we picked the burrs out of my hair.

Granpa said he *knowed* ol' Slick would pull that trick, and that's why he chose the place for us to set. He said that, without a doubt, ol' Slick had set close by and watched the dogs his own self.

Granpa said the reason ol' Slick had waited so long for the hounds to get close is that he wanted his scent to be fresh on the rocks, figuring that the hounds' *feelings* would take over from their *sense*, when they got excited. It worked too, with ol' Rippitt and Bess; but not with Blue Boy and Little Red.

Granpa said he had many's the time seen that same kind of thing, feelings taking over sense, make as big a fools out of people as it had ol' Rippitt. Which I reckin is so.

It had broke day and I hadn't even noticed. Me and Granpa moved down to the creek bank clearing and et our sour biscuits and meat. The dogs was baying back around and coming along the ridge in front of us.

The sun topped the mountain, sparkling the trees across the creek and brought out brush wrens and a red cardinal.

Granpa slid his knife under the bark of a cedar tree and made a dipper by twisting one end of the bark. We dipped water from the creek, cold, where you could see the pebbles on the bottom. The water had a cedary taste that made me hungrier, but we had et all the biscuits.

Granpa said ol' Slick *might* come up the farther creek bank this time, and we would get to see him again; but we would have to sit quiet. I didn't move, not even when the ants crawled up on my foot, though I wanted to. Granpa saw them, and said it was all right to brush them off—ol' Slick wouldn't see me do that. Which I did.

In a little while the hounds were below us again, down the creek, and then we saw him, lazying up the creek bank on the other side with his tongue hanging out. Granpa give a low whistle and ol' Slick stopped and stared across the creek at us. He stood there a minute, with his eyes crinkled up like he was grinning at us; then he snorted and trotted on out of sight.

Granpa said ol' Slick snorted because he was disgusted, being caused all this inconvenience. I remembered ol' Slick had it coming to him.

Granpa said some fellers told that they had heard about foxes "swapping out," but he had actually seen it. He said years ago, he had been fox trailing and was sittin' on a hillock above a meadow clearing. He said the fox, a red one, come along with the hounds behind him and stopped at a hollow tree and give a little bark. He said another fox come out of that hollow tree, and the first one got in. Then the second fox trotted off, leading the dogs on the trail. He said he moved close to that tree and could hear that ol' fox actually *snoring* while the hounds was passing a few feet from him. He said that ol' fox had so much confidence in hisself that he didn't give a lick-damn *how* close them dogs come around him.

Here comes Blue Boy and the pack up the creek bank. They bayed every step or two . . . it was a strong trail. They passed out of sight and in a minute, one bay split off from the rest and broke up into yelps and howls.

Granpa cussed. He said, "Damn! Ol' Rippitt is trying to

cut acrost again and cheat on ol' Slick. He's gone and got
hisself lost." In the mountains, such is known as a "cheater
hound."

Granpa said we would have to set up a hollering and
baying ourselves to guide ol' Rippitt back to us, and that
would call off the trailing, because the other dogs would
come too. So we did.

I couldn't give the long holler like Granpa—it was
almost like a yodel—but I did tolerable well, Granpa said.

In a little while here they come, and ol' Rippitt was
ashamed of what he had done. He hung back behind the
others; hoping, I reckin, that he would pass unnoticed.
Granpa said it served him right and maybe *this* time it
would learn him that you can't cheat without making unnecessary trouble for yourself. Which proves out as reasonable.

The sun had slanted into the afternoon when we left
Hangin' Gap, back down the Narrows toward home. The
dogs dragged their feet in the trail and I knew they were
tired. I was too and would have had a hard time making it
if Granpa hadn't been so tuckered that he walked along
slow.

It was dusk evening when we sighted the cabin clearing
and Granma. She was out on the trail to meet us. She
picked me up, though I could have made it, and put an
arm around Granpa's waist. I guess I was tuckered, for I
fell asleep on her shoulder and didn't know when we got
to the cabin.

"I Kin Ye, Bonnie Bee"

LOOKING BACK, I guess me and Granpa was pretty dumb. Not Granpa, when it come to mountains or game or weather or any number of things. But when you got into words and books and such, well, me and Granpa took the decision to Granma. She straightened it out.

Like the time the lady asked us for directions.

We had been to the settlement and was on our way back home, and pretty heavy loaded. We had so many books that we split them up. Granpa was put out about the number of books. He said the librarian was pushing too many on us every month, and he was getting different people tangled up in the stories.

For the past month he had been arguing that Alexander the Great sided with the big bankers at the Continental Congress and tried to undercut Mr. Jefferson. Granma had been telling him that Alexander the Great was not politicking at that time, and as a matter of fact, was not living at that time. But Granpa had it stuck in his mind, so we had to get the book back on Alexander the Great.

Granpa was tolerable sure that the book would prove out as to what Granma said. I was tolerable sure myself as I had never known Granma to miss when it come to knowing what was in books.

So, in the back of our minds, all the time, we knew Granma was right and Granpa had come down pretty heavy on the idea that it was getting too many books that was the *cause* of the confusion. Which sounded reasonable to me.

Anyhow, I was carrying one of Mr. Shakespeare's books and the dictionary, along with the can of coal oil. Granpa had the rest of the books and a can of coffee. Granma loved coffee and I figured, like Granpa, that the coffee would help out when we got to Alexander the Great, for the entire thing had been a worriment to Granma for the solid month.

We was on the road from the settlement, me walking behind Granpa, when a big black car pulled up beside us and stopped. It was the biggest car I had ever seen. There were two ladies and two men in the car, and it had glass windows that slid right down into the door.

I had never seen such before, nor had Granpa, for we both watched the window while it slid out of sight as the lady cranked on it. Later, Granpa told me that he inspected it right close and there was a narrow slit in the door that allowed the glass to go down. I didn't see it, for I was not tall enough.

The lady was fine dressed with rings on her fingers and big bobbles that hung down from her ears.

"Which way do we go to get to Chattanooga?" she asked, and you couldn't hardly hear the motor running on the car.

Granpa set the coffee can down on the ground and balanced his books on top of it so they wouldn't get dirty. I set down my coal oil can; for Granpa always said that if you was spoken to, treat such with proper respect and give full attention to what was being said. After we had done that, Granpa lifted his hat to the lady, which seemed like it made her feel bad for she hollered at Granpa, "I *said*, which way do we go to get to Chattanooga? Are you *deef?*"

Granpa said, "No, ma'am, my hearin' and health is fine today, thank ye. How's your'n?" And Granpa meant it; for it was custom to inquire about such as how people was feeling. Me and Granpa was a little surprised when the woman acted like it made her mad, but that could have been because the other folks in the car was laughing at something she must have done.

She hollered louder, "Are you going to *tell* us how to get to Chattanooga?"

"Why yes, ma'am," Granpa said.

"*Well*," the lady said, "*tell* us!"

"Well," Granpa said, "first off, ye're headed wrong, which is east. Ye want to go west. Now not dead west, but sly off jest a shade to the north, about where that big ridge is, over yonder . . . and that ought to take ye there." Granpa lifted his hat again, and we bent to take up our loads.

The lady stuck her head out of the window. "Are you for *real*?" she hollered. "What *road* do we take?"

Granpa straightened up, surprised. "Why, I reckin whichever one goes west, ma'am—bearing in mind to sly off toward the north."

"What are you, a couple of *foreigners*?" the lady hollered.

Now this set Granpa back; it did me too, for I had never heard that word, and I don't think Granpa had either. He looked at the lady for a dead minute, and then he said, real firm, "I reckin."

The big car taken off, still headed the way it had been going, which was east, and the wrong way. Granpa shook his head and said in his seventy-odd years, he had struck up with some crazy people, but the lady proved up to any of them. I asked Granpa if she could have been a politician, but he said he had never heard of a lady being a politician —though she could have been the wife of one.

We turned off onto the wagon ruts. Always, on the way back from the settlement, when we got on the wagon ruts, I commenced to think of something to ask Granpa. He always stopped when he was spoken to, as I say, to give full consideration to whatever was said. This gave me a chance to catch up. I reckin I was little for my age (five going on six) for the top of my head come just above Granpa's knees, and I was always in a continual trot behind him.

I had fallen back a good ways and was trotting hard, so I had to might near holler, "Granpa, have ye ever been to Chattanooga?"

Granpa stopped. "Noooo," he said, "but I nearly went there oncet." I caught up and set down my coal oil can.

"Must have been twenty . . . maybe thirty years ago, I reckin," Granpa said. "I had an uncle, Enoch was his name, youngest of Pa's brothers. He was gittin' age on him, and when he liquored up would ofttimes git addled in the head and wander off. Well, Uncle Enoch disappeared which he oft did on high lonesomes, back in the mountains, but this time it stretched out to three er four weeks. Set us to sending inquiries with travelers. Word come back that he was in Chattanooga, in jail. I was set to go and fetch him out, when he showed up at the cabin."

Granpa paused to give thought to it, and begun to laugh. "Yessir, he showed up barefooted, with nothing but some old floppy britches on that he had to hold up with one hand. He looked like he had been set upon by boar 'coons . . . he was that skint up. Turned out, he had walked back ever step of the way through the mountains." Granpa stopped to laugh, and I set down on the coal oil can, which rested my legs.

"Uncle Enoch said he had got liquored up and didn't recollect about how he got there; but he woke up in a room in a bed with two women. He said he had just commenced to climb out of bed and disassociate hisself from them when a banging set up on the door and a big feller busted in. The feller was mad and said one of the women was his wife and the other'n was his sister. Seems like Uncle Enoch had somehow or other got associated with practical the entire family.

"Uncle Enoch said the women set up and commenced to holler fer him to pay the feller something, and said the feller was hollering, and Uncle Enoch was casting about trying to find his pants. Though he doubted there was any money in the pockets, he knowed he had a cuttin' knife; fer the feller 'peared like he meant business. But he couldn't find his pants, having no way in the world of knowing what he done with them, and there was nothing else fer him to do so he leapt out a window. Trouble was, the window was two stories up, and Uncle Enoch hit spraddled out in gravel and rock; that's how he got skint up.

"He hadn't a stitch of clothes on, but he found a window shade, having brought it down with him. He said he wrapped the window shade 'round his private parts, and set about to hide until dark. Trouble was, he couldn't find no place to hide; stepped out slap in the middle of a bunch of folks rushing around this-a-way and that. He said they had no manners atall and he liked to got run over twicet. The law got him and put him in jail.

"The next morning, they give him some pants and a shirt and shoes too big fer him, and put him out with some more fellers sweeping up the streets. Uncle Enoch said they was less than a round dozen of them, all told, doing the sweeping, and he didn't see any way in the world they could ever git that place cleaned up. He said people was throwing things down on the streets faster than they could sweep it up. He said he saw no point atall to the thing, and determined he would leave. First chancet he got, he broke and run. Feller grabbed his shirt, but he run out of it; run out'n his shoes too, but he held up his pants. He said he run into some trees and hid out 'til dark, when he got his bearings by the stars and struck out fer home. Taken him three weeks to make it acrost the mountains, grazing on acorns and hickor'nuts like a hog. Cured Uncle Enoch's liquoring . . . wouldn't never go near a settlement again, far as I know. Nope," Granpa said, "I never been to Chattanooga; ain't goin' neither."

I made up my mind right then that I wasn't ever going to Chattanooga myself.

We was at supper that night when it crossed my mind to ask Granma, and so I said, "Granma, what is foreigners?"

Granpa stopped eating, but he didn't look up from his plate. Granma looked at me and then at Granpa. Her eyes twinkled. "Well," she said, "foreigners is people that happen to be someplace where they wasn't born."

"Granpa said," I explained, "that he reckined we was foreigners." And I told about the lady in the big car and how she had said we was foreigners, and Granpa said he reckined. Granpa pushed his plate back. "I reckined that we wasn't borned down there on the side of the road, which made us foreigners to them parts. Anyhow it's another one of them dadblamed words [he always used "dadblamed" instead of "damn" in front of Granma] that we can do without. There is, I have always said, too dadblamed many words."

Granma agreed that there was. Granma didn't want to get into the word business. She had never, for example, got the words "knowed" and "throwed" disentangled with Granpa. He said that "knew" was something you got which nobody had ever used, and that the word, therefore, was "knowed." And he said "threw" was how you got from one side of a door to the other side, and therefore it was "throwed." He wouldn't budge on it, as what he said made sense.

Granpa said if there was less words, there wouldn't be as much trouble in the world. He said privately to me that there was always some damn fool making up a word that served no purpose except to cause trouble. Which is reasonable. Granpa favored the *sound*, or how you said a word, as to its meaning. He said folks that spoke different words could feel the same thing by listening to the *sound* of music. Granma agreed with him, because that's the way they talked to each other.

Granma's name was Bonnie Bee. I knew that when I heard him late at night say, "I kin ye, Bonnie Bee," he was saying, "I love ye," for the feeling was in the words.

And when they would be talking and Granma would say, "Do ye kin me, Wales?" and he would answer, "I kin ye," it meant, "I understand ye." To them, love and understanding was the same thing. Granma said you couldn't love something you didn't understand; nor could you love people, nor God, if you didn't understand the people and God.

Granpa and Granma had an understanding, and so they had a love. Granma said the understanding run deeper as the years went by, and she reckined it would get beyond anything mortal folks could think upon or explain. And so they called it "kin."

Granpa said back before his time "kinfolks" meant any folks that you understood and had an understanding with, so it meant "loved folks." But people got selfish, and brought it down to mean just blood relatives; but that actually it was never meant to mean that.

Granpa said when he was a little boy his Pa had a friend who ofttimes hung around their cabin. He said he was an old Cherokee named 'Coon Jack, and he was continually distempered and cantankerous. He couldn't figure out what his Pa saw in old 'Coon Jack.

He said they went irregular to a little church house down in a hollow. One Sunday it was testifying time, when folks would stand up, as they felt the Lord called on them, and testify as to their sins and how much they loved the Lord.

Granpa said at this testifying time, "'Coon Jack stood up and said, 'I hear tell they's some in here been talking about me behind my back. I want ye to know that I'm awares. I know what's the matter with ye; ye're jealous because the Deacon Board put me in charge of the key to the songbook box. Well, let me tell ye; any of ye don't like it, I got the difference right here in my pocket.'"

Granpa said, shore enough, 'Coon Jack lifted his deer shirt and showed a pistol handle. He was stomping mad.

Granpa said that church house was full of some hard men, including his Pa, who would soon as not shoot you if the weather changed, but nobody raised an eyebrow. He said his Pa stood up and said, " 'Coon Jack, every man here admires the way ye have handled the key to the songbook box. Best handling ever been done. If words has been mistook to cause ye discomfort, I here and now state the sorrow of every man present."

'Coon Jack set down, total mollified and contented, as was everybody else.

On the way home, Granpa asked his Pa why 'Coon Jack could get away with such talk, and Granpa said he got to laughing about 'Coon Jack acting so important over the key to the songbook box. He said his Pa told him, "Son, don't laugh at 'Coon Jack. Ye see, when the Cherokee was forced to give up his home and go to the Nations, 'Coon Jack was young, and he hid out in these mountains and he fought to hold on. When the War 'tween tne States come, he saw maybe he could fight that same guvmin. and get back the land and homes. He fought hard. Both times he lost. When the War ended, the politicians set in, trying to git what was left of what we had. 'Coon Jack fought, and run, and hid, and fought some more. Ye see, 'Coon Jack come up in the time of fighting. All he's got now is the key to the songbook box. And if 'Coon Jack seems cantankerous . . . well, there ain't nothing left for 'Coon Jack to fight. He never knowed nothing else."

Granpa said, he come might near crying fer 'Coon Jack. He said after that, it didn't matter what 'Coon Jack said, or did . . . he loved him, because he understood him.

Granpa said that such was "kin," and most of people's mortal trouble come about by not practicing it; from that and politicians.

I could see that right off, and might near cried about 'Coon Jack myself.

To Know the Past

GRANMA AND GRANPA wanted me to know of the past, for "If ye don't know the past, then ye will not have a future. If ye don't know where your people have been, then ye won't know where your people are going." And so they told me most of it.

How the government soldiers came. How the Cherokee had farmed the rich valleys and held their mating dances in the spring when life was planted in the ground; when the buck and doe, the cock and peahen exulted in the creation parts they played.

How their harvest festivals were held in the villages as frost turned the pumpkins, reddened the persimmon and hardened the corn. How they prepared for the winter hunts and pledged themselves to The Way.

How the government soldiers came, and told them to sign the paper. Told them the paper meant that the new white settlers would know where they could settle and where they would not take land of the Cherokee. And after they had signed it, more government soldiers came with guns and long knives fixed on their guns. The soldiers said the paper had changed its words. The words now said that the Cherokee must give up his valleys, his homes and his mountains. He must go far toward the setting sun, where the government had other land for the Cherokee, land that the white man did not want.

How the government soldiers came, and ringed a big valley with their guns, and at night with their campfires. They put the Cherokees in the ring. They brought Cherokees in from other mountains and valleys, in bunches like cattle, and put them in the ring.

After a long time of this, when they had most of the Cherokees, they brought wagons and mules and told the Cherokees they could ride to the land of the setting sun. The Cherokees had nothing left. But they would not ride, and so they saved something. You could not see it or wear it or eat it, but they saved something; and they would not ride. They walked.

Government soldiers rode before them, on each side of them, behind them. The Cherokee men walked and looked straight ahead and would not look down, nor at the soldiers. Their women and their children followed in their footsteps and would not look at the soldiers.

Far behind them, the empty wagons rattled and rumbled and served no use. The wagons could not steal the soul of the Cherokee. The land was stolen from him, his home; but the Cherokee would not let the wagons steal his soul.

As they passed the villages of the white man, people lined the trail to watch them pass. At first, they laughed at how foolish was the Cherokee to walk with the empty wagons rattling behind him. The Cherokee did not turn his head at their laughter, and soon there was no laughter.

And as the Cherokee walked farther from his mountains, he began to die. His soul did not die, nor did it weaken. It was the very young and the very old and the sick.

At first the soldiers let them stop to bury their dead; but then, more died—by the hundreds—by the thousands. More than a third of them were to die on the Trail. The soldiers said they could only bury their dead every three days; for the soldiers wished to hurry and be finished with the Cherokee. The soldiers said the wagons would carry the dead, but the Cherokee would not put his dead in the wagons. He carried them. Walking.

The little boy carried his dead baby sister, and slept by her at night on the ground. He lifted her in his arms in the morning, and carried her.

The husband carried his dead wife. The son carried his dead mother, his father. The mother carried her dead baby. They carried them in their arms. And walked. And they did not turn their heads to look at the soldiers, nor to look at the people who lined the sides of the Trail to watch them pass. Some of the people cried. But the Cherokee did not cry. Not on the outside, for the Cherokee would not let them see his soul; as he would not ride in the wagons.

And so they called it the Trail of Tears. Not because the Cherokee cried; for he did not. They called it the Trail of Tears for it sounds romantic and speaks of the sorrow of those who stood by the Trail. A death march is not romantic.

You cannot write poetry about the death-stiffened baby in his mother's arms, staring at the jolting sky with eyes that will not close; while his mother walks.

You cannot sing songs of the father laying down the burden of his wife's corpse, to lie by it through the night and to rise and carry it again in the morning—and tell his oldest son to carry the body of his youngest. And do not look . . . nor speak . . . nor cry . . . nor remember the mountains.

It would not be a beautiful song. And so they call it the Trail of Tears.

All of the Cherokee did not go. Some, skilled in the ways of mountains, fled far back into the bosom of her hollows, the raceways of her ridges, and lived with their women and children, always moving.

They set traps for game but sometimes dared not go

back to the traps, for the soldiers had come. They dug the
sweet root from the ground, pounded the acorn into meal,
cut poke salat from the clearings, and pulled the inner
bark from the tree. They fished with their hands under
the banks of the cold creeks and moved silent as shadows,
a people who were there but not seen (except by a flicker
of illusion), not heard; and they left little signs of their
living.

But here and there they found friends. The people of
Granpa's Pa were mountain bred. They did not lust for
land, or profit, but loved the freedom of the mountains,
as did the Cherokee.

Granma told how Granpa's Pa had met his wife,
Granpa's Ma, and her people. He had seen the faintest
of signs on the banks of a creek. He had gone home and
brought back a haunch of deer and laid it there in a little
clearing. With it, he had laid his gun and his knife. The
next morning he came back. The deer haunch was gone,
but the gun and the knife were there, and lying beside
them was another knife, a long Indian knife, and a tomahawk. He did not take them. Instead he brought ears of
corn and laid them by the weapons; he stood and waited
a long time.

They came slowly in the late afternoon. Moving through
the trees and halting and then coming forward again.
Granpa's Pa reached out his hands, and they, a dozen of
them—men, women, children—reached out their hands
and they touched. Granma said they each had to reach
across a long way to do it, but they did.

Granpa's Pa grew up tall and married the youngest of
the daughters. They held the hickory marriage stick together and put it in their cabin, and neither of them
broke it as long as they lived. She wore the feather of the
red-winged blackbird in her hair, and so was called Red
Wing. Granma said she was slender as a willow wand and
sang in the evenings.

Granma and Granpa spoke of his Pa in his last years.

He was an old warrior. He had joined the Confederate raider, John Hunt Morgan, to fight the faraway, faceless monster of "guvmint," that threatened his people and his cabin.

His beard was white. Age was overtaking his gauntness; and now when the winter wind bit through the cracks of his cabin, the old hurts came to life. The saber slash that ran the length of his left arm; the steel had hit the bone, like a meat axe. The flesh had healed, but the bone marrow thumped with pain and reminded him of the "guvmint" men.

He had downed half a jug that night in Kain'tuck, while the boys heated a ramrod over the fire and seared the wound and stopped the blood. He had climbed back in the saddle.

The ankle was the worst of it. He hated the ankle. It was big and cumbersome where the minnie ball had chewed it in passing. He hadn't noticed it at the time. It had been the wild exuberance of a cavalry charge that night in Ohio. The fever for combat, that marked his breed, was running high. There was no fear, only exultation, as the horse moved fast and light over the ground, as the wind whipped a storm in his face. Exultation that brought the rebel Indian yell rumbling from his chest and out his throat, screaming, savage.

That's why a man could get half his leg mangled and not know it. Not until twenty miles farther on, when they reconnoitered in the dark of a mountain hollow, and he stepped from the saddle and his leg buckled under him, the blood sloshing in his boot like a full well bucket, did he notice the ankle.

He relished thinking of that charge. The memory of it softened his hatred for the cane—and the limp.

The worst of the hurts was in the gut; in his side, near the hip. That's where the lead was never taken out. It gnawed, like a rat chewing at a corn crib, night and day;

and never stopped. It was eating away at his insides; and soon now, they would stretch him out on the floor of the mountain cabin and cut him open, like a butchered bull.

The putridness would come out; the gangrene. They would not use anesthetics, just a swig from the mountain jug. And he would die there on the floor, in his blood. No last words; but as they held his arms and legs in the death throes, the old sinewy body would bow up from the floor, and the wild scream of the exulting rebel's challenge to hated government would come from his throat and he would die. Forty years it had taken the "guvmint" lead to kill him.

The century was dying. The time of blood and fighting and death; the time he had met, and by which he had been measured, was dying. There would be a new century, with another people marching and carrying their dead, but he knew only the past—of the Cherokee.

His oldest son had ridden off to the Nations; the next oldest dead in Texas. Now, only Red Wing, as in the beginning, and his youngest son.

He could still ride. He could jump a Morgan horse over a five-rail fence. He still bobbed the horses' tails, out of habit, to leave no tail hair on the brush to be followed.

But the pains were worse and the jug didn't quieten them as it had. He was coming to the time of being spread-eagled on the floor of the cabin. And he knew it.

The fall of year was dying in the Tennessee mountains. The wind bit the last of the leaves from hickory and oak. He stood, that winter afternoon with his son, halfway down the hollow; not admitting that he couldn't climb the mountain anymore.

They watched the naked trees, stark on the ridge against the sky; as though they were studying the winter slant of sun. They would not look at each other.

"Reckin I'll not be leavin' ye much," he said, and laughed soft, "best ye could git from that cabin would be to touch a lighter knot to it fer a hand warming." His son studied the mountain. "I reckin," he said quietly.

"Ye're a man, full and with family," the old man said, "and I'll not hold ye to a lot . . . 'ceptin' we stretch our hand to clasp any man's as quick as we'll defend what we was give to believe. My time is gone, and now the time will be something I don't know, fer you. I wouldn't know how to live in it . . . no more'n 'Coon Jack. Mind ye've little to meet it with . . . but the mountains'll not change on ye, and ye kin them; and we be honest men with our feelings."

"I mind," the son said. The weak sun had set behind the ridge, and the wind bit sharp. It came hard for the old man to say . . . but he did. ". . . and . . . I . . . kin ye, son."

The son did not speak, but he slipped his arm around the old, skinny shoulders. The shadows of the hollow were deep now and blurred the mountains black on either side of them. They walked slowly in this fashion, the old man touching his cane to the ground, down the hollow to the cabin.

It was the last walk and talk Granpa had with his Pa. I have been many times to their graves; close together, high on a ridge of white oak, where the leaves fall knee-deep in autumn, until they are whipped away by mean winter winds. Where only the hardiest Indian violets poke tiny and blue around them in the spring, timid in their presence before the fierce and lasting souls who weathered their time.

The marriage stick is there, hickory and gnarled, un-broken still, and filled with the notches they carved in it each time they had a sorrow, a happiness, a quarrel they had mended. It rests at their heads, holding them together.

And so small are the carved names in the stick, you must get down on your knees to read: Ethan and Red Wing.

Pine Billy

IN THE WINTERTIME, we carried leaves and put them on the corn patch. Back in the hollow, past the barn, the corn patch flattened out on either side of the spring branch. Granpa had cleared it a little ways up the sides of the mountain. The "slants," as Granpa called the sloping sides of the corn patch, didn't raise good corn, but he planted it anyhow. There wasn't much flat ground in the hollow.

I liked gathering the leaves and putting them in the tow sacks. They were light to carry. Me and Granpa and Granma would help each other fill the sacks. Granpa would carry two, and sometimes three sacks. I tried to carry two, but couldn't make much headway at it. Knee-deep for me, the leaves were like a brown snowfall on the ground, dappled with the yellow paint of maple leaves, and the red of bee gum and sumach bushes.

We would come out of the woods and scatter the leaves over the field. Pine straw too. Granpa said some pine straw was necessary to acid the ground—but not too much.

We never worked so long or hard that it got tedious. We usually was "drawed off," as Granpa put it, to something else.

Granma would see yellowroot and dig that up; and that

led her to some ginseng, or iron root . . . or calum . . . or sassafras . . . or lady's slipper. She knew them all, and had a remedy for any ailment of which I have ever heard. Her remedies worked too; though some of the tonics I would as soon not have drunk.

Me and Granpa usually run across hickor'nuts, or chinkapins and chestnuts; sometimes black walnuts. It wasn't that we special *looked* for them, it just seemed to happen. Between our eating and gathering nuts and roots, and seeing a 'coon or watching a peckerwood, our leaf carrying would get down to practical nothing.

As we would walk down the hollow in evening dusk, all of us loaded with nuts and roots and such, Granpa would cuss under his breath where Granma couldn't hear him, and then he'd announce that next time we was not going to get "drawed off" to such foolishness; and were going to spend the whole time carrying leaves. Which always sounded mighty dismal to me; but it never happened.

Sack by sack, we got the field covered with leaves and pine straw. And after a light rain, when the leaves clung to the ground just enough, Granpa would hitch up ol' Sam, the mule, to the plow; and we turned the leaves under the ground.

I say "we," because Granpa let me plow some. I had to reach up over my head to hold the handles of the plow stock, and spent most of my time pulling all my weight down on the handles to keep the plow point from going too deep into the ground. Sometimes the point would come out of the ground, and the plow would skitter along, not plowing. Ol' Sam was patient with me. He would stop while I pulled and strained at getting the plow upright, and then would move ahead when I said, "Giddup!"

I had to push up on the handles to make the plow point go into the ground; and so, between the pulling down and the pushing up, I learned to keep my chin away from the crossbar between the handles, for I was getting continual licks that jolted me up pretty bad.

Granpa followed along behind us, but he would let me do it. If you wanted ol' Sam to move to the left, you said, "Haw!" and if you wanted him to move to the right, you said, "Gee!" ol' Sam would meander off a little to the left and I would holler, "Gee!"; but he was hard of hearing and would keep meandering. Granpa would take it up, "Gee! Gee! GEE! DAMMITOHELL! GEE!" and ol' Sam would come back to the right.

Trouble was, ol' Sam heard this so much, that he begun to connect up the total geeing and the cussing, and would not go right until he heard all of it; figuring natural, that to go right, it took the whole amount. This led to considerable cussing, which I had to take up in order to plow. This was all right until Granma heard me and spoke hard to Granpa about it. This cut down on my plowing considerable when Granma was around.

Ol' Sam was blind in his left eye, so when he reached the end of the field, he would not turn around going to his left, figuring he might bump into something. He would always turn to his right. When you're plowing, turning to the right works good at one end of the field; but at the other, it seems you have to turn a full circle, dragging the plow completely out of the field into bushes and briers and such. Granpa said we had to be patient with ol' Sam, as he was old and half-blind, so I was, but I dreaded every other turn at the end of the field; especially when there was a thicket of blackberry bushes waiting on me.

One time, Granpa was pulling and dragging the plow around through a mass of nettles, and stepped in a stump hole. It was a warm day, and yellow jackets had a nest in that hole. They got up Granpa's britches leg and he taken off hollering for the spring branch. I saw the yellow jackets come out, and I taken off too. Granpa flattened out in the spring branch, slapping at his britches and cussing ol' Sam. He might near lost his patience.

But ol' Sam stood patient and waited until Granpa got over it. Trouble was, we couldn't get near the plow. The yellow jackets was all stirred up and swarming around that plow. Me and Granpa got out in the middle of the field and Granpa would try to get ol' Sam to come forward, away from the yellow jacket nest.

Granpa would call, "Come on, Sam—come on, boy," but ol' Sam wouldn't move. He knew his business and he knew better than to pull a plow laying sidewise on the ground. Granpa tried everything; a considerable cussing, and he got down on all fours and brayed like a mule. I thought he brayed tolerable close to the sound of a mule; and once, ol' Sam leaned his ears forward and looked hard at Granpa, but he wouldn't move. I tried braying myself, but I couldn't touch Granpa's bray. When Granpa saw Granma had come up and was watching us on all fours in the middle of the field and braying, he quit.

He had to go into the woods and get a lighter knot, which he touched a match to and pitched in the stump hole. This smoked the yellow jackets away from the plow.

Going back to the cabin that evening, Granpa said it had been a worrisome puzzlement to him for many years whether ol' Sam was the dumbest mule in the world, or the smartest. I never figured it out myself.

I liked the field plowing, though. It growed me up. When we walked down the trail to the cabin, it 'peared to me that my steps was lengthening quite some bit behind Granpa. Granpa bragged on me a lot to Granma at the supper table and Granma agreed that it looked like I was coming on to being a man.

We were at the supper table one such evening, when the hounds set up a racket. We all went out to the front porch to see a man coming across the foot log. He was a fine looking feller, nearly tall as Granpa. I liked his shoes the best, they was bright yellow, high top, with white socks rolled around and lump tied to hold them up. His overalls struck him just above the socks. He had on a short black coat and a white shirt and had a little hat that set square

on his head. He was carrying a long case. Granma and
Granpa knew him.

"Well, it's Pine Billy," Granpa said. Pine Billy waved.
"Come in and stay awhile," Granpa said.

Pine Billy stopped at the doorstep. "Aw, I was just
passing by," he said . . . and I wondered where he was
passing to, with just mountains behind us.

"Ye're goin' to stay and eat with us," Granma said, and
got Pine Billy by the arm and led him up the doorsteps.
Granpa taken his long case by the handle, and we all
went in the kitchen.

I could tell right off that Granpa and Granma liked Pine
Billy a lot. He had four sweet 'taters in his coat pockets
and gave them to Granma. She made them into a pie right
then, and Pine Billy et three pieces of it. I got one, and
was hoping he would not eat the last piece. We moved
away from the table to set by the fireplace and left the
piece of pie in a pan on the table.

Pine Billy laughed a whole lot and said I was going to
be bigger'n Granpa. Which made me feel good. He said
Granma was purtier'n the last time he'd seen her, and
this pleased Granma; Granpa too. I commenced to feel
right good about Pine Billy, even if he had et the three
pieces of pie—they was his 'taters.

We all set around the fire. Granma in her rocker and
Granpa leaning forward in his. I figured something was
up. Granpa asked, "Well, what's the news. Pine Billy, that
ye hear around?"

Pine Billy leaned back on two legs of the straight-back
chair. He took a finger and thumb and pulled out his lower
lip and turned a little can upward, putting snuff in his lip.
He offered the can to Granpa and Granma. They shook
their heads. Pine Billy was sure taking his time. He spit in
the fire. "Well," he said, "look's like I might have come up
on something that'll fix me in good shape." He spit in
the fire again and looked around at all of us.

I didn't know what it was, but I could tell it was important.

Granpa figured it was too, for he asked, "What is it, Pine Billy?" Pine Billy leaned back again and looked at the roof rafters. He clasped his hands across his stomach.

"Must'a been last Wednesday . . . nooo, it was a'Tuesday, fer I'd been playin' at a Jumpin' Jody dance on a'Monday night; Tuesday it was. I come through the settlement on a'Tuesday. Ye know the po-liceman there, Smokehouse Turner?"

"Yes, yes, I've seed him," Granpa said, impatient.

"Well," Pine Billy said, "I was standing on the corner there, talking to Smokehouse, when this big, shiny car pulled into the fillin' station acrost the road. Smokehouse didn't notice it . . . but I did. It had one feller in it, and he was dressed fit to kill; big city. He got out of his car and told Joe Holcomb to fill it up with gasoline. Well, I was watchin' 'em, all the time; and he looked around, kind'a sneaky. It hit me right off. I says to myself, 'That's a big-city CRIMINAL.' Mind ye," Pine Billy said, "I didn't say it to Smokehouse. I jest said it to m'self. But to Smokehouse I says, 'Smokehouse, ye know I'm agin turning anybody in to the law . . . but big-city criminals is different, and that feller over there looks total suspicious to me.'

"Smokehouse studied the feller and says, 'Ye could be right, Pine Billy. We'll jest have a look,' and he ambles acrost the road to the feller's car."

Pine Billy brought his chair down on four legs and spit in the fire and studied the logs a minute. I couldn't hardly wait to hear what happened to the criminal.

Pine Billy finished studying the logs and said, "Now ye know, Smokehouse cain't read ner write, and as I can make out lettering right fair, I follered him over, in case I was needed. The feller seen us comin' and got back in his car. We walked up and Smokehouse leaned on his

winder and asked him politely what he was doing in the
settlement. The feller was nervous, I could see, and said
he was on his way to Floridy. Which sounded suspicious."

It sounded suspicious to me too, and I seen Granpa nod
his head.

Pine Billy continued, "Smokehouse said, 'Where are ye
from?' The feller said he was from Chicargo. Smokehouse
said he reckined that was all right, but fer the feller to
git on out of the settlement, and the feller agreed that he
would. Now in the meantime . . ." Pine Billy cocked his
eyes around at Granpa and Granma ". . . in the meantime,
I edged back behind the car and lettered out his tag plate.
I pulled Smokehouse aside, and I told him, 'He says he's
from Chicargo, but—he's got a Illinoys tag on his car.'
Ol' Smokehouse was on him like a bottle fly on syrup. He
pulled that criminal out'n his car and stood him up aside
of it, and asked him flat out . . . 'If ye're from Chicargo,
what are ye doin' with Illinoys tag on yer car?' Smokehouse
knowed he had him. It caught the criminal flat-footed; he
didn't know what to say; caught 'em in a barefaced lie, ye
see. He tried to slick talk his way out'n it, but I'll say this
fer ol' Smokehouse, he ain't all that easy to slicker."

Pine Billy was plumb excited now. "Smokehouse put the
criminal in jail and said he would check it out; probably a
big reward, and I'll git half of it. From the looks of the
feller, it might be a bigger reward than me and Smokehouse either one has figgered."

Granma and Granpa both agreed that it sounded mighty
promising and Granpa said he didn't hold with big-city
criminals. Which I don't neither. We all saw pretty plain
that Pine Billy was as good as rich.

But Pine Billy wasn't uppity about it. He said there
could be the possibility that it wouldn't amount to a very
big reward. He never put all his eggs in one basket, ner
counted his chickens before they hatched. Which is
sensible.

He said he had done some work on something else, just in case. He said the Red Eagle snuff company was holding a contest that paid five hundred dollars to the winner—practical enough to set a man up fer life. He said he had got hold of a entering paper and all you had to do was tell why you liked Red Eagle snuff. He said he labored over it before he filled it in, and come up with what he figured was the winningest answer that could be thought of.

Pine Billy said that most folks entering would say that Red Eagle was good snuff, and he said that too; but he went farther than that. He said he put down that it was the *best* snuff of any he had put in his mouth; and further-more, he would *never* put any other kind of snuff in his mouth but Red Eagle, as long as he lived. He said that he used his head, because when the big men at the Red Eagle snuff company see that, then they would *know* they would eventually git all their money back, seeing as how Pine Billy would be continually using their snuff for the rest of his life. If they give the money to somebody that just said Red Eagle was good, and let it go at that, well, they was takin' a chance.

Pine Billy said them big fellers didn't take no chances, not with their money; that was why they was rich. He figured he pretty well had the Red Eagle proposition practically in his pocket.

Granpa agreed the money looked right certain. Pine Billy went to the door and spit out his snuff. He come back by the table and got the piece of sweet 'tater pie. I didn't mind as bad—though I still wanted it—but seein' as Pine Billy was rich, he probably deserved it.

Granpa got out his stone jug and Pine Billy took two or three swigs and Granpa took one. Granma coughed and got her jug of cough syrup. Granpa got Pine Billy to get his fiddle and bow, and play "Red Wing." Granpa and Granma tapped their feet. He sure could play pretty, and he sung it too:

"Now the moon shines tonight, on pretty Red Wing,
The breezes sighing; the night birds crying
While afar 'neath the stars, her brave is sleeping
While Red Wing's weeping, her heart away."

I went to sleep on the floor and Granma carried me to
bed. Last I heard was the fiddle. I dreamed that Pine
Billy came to our cabin and he was rich and had a tow
sack on his shoulder. It was full of sweet 'taters.

The Secret Place

RECKIN A MILLION little critters live along the spring branch.

If you could be a giant and could look down on its bends and curves, you would know the spring branch is a river of life.

I was the giant. Being over two feet tall, I squatted, giant-like, to study the little marshes where trickles of the stream eddied off into low places. Frogs laid eggs; big crystal balls of jelly that had pollywogs dotted all through them . . . waiting for the time to eat their way out.

Rock minnows darted to chase musk bugs scuttering across the stream. When you held a musk bug in your hand, it smelled real sweet and thick.

Once I spent a whole afternoon collecting some musk bugs, just a few in my pocket, for they are hard to catch. I took them to Granma, as I knew she loved sweet smells. She always put honeysuckle in her lye soap when she made it.

She was more excited about the musk bugs than I was, might near. She said she had never smelled anything so sweet and couldn't figger how she had missed out on knowing about musk bugs.

At the supper table she told Granpa about it before I could, and how it was the brandest new thing she had ever smelled. Granpa was struck dumfounded. I let him smell of them and he said he had lived seventy odd years, total unaware of such a smell.

Granma said I had done right, for when you come on something that is good, first thing to do is share it with whoever you can find; that way, the good spreads out to where no telling it will go. Which is right.

I got pretty wet, splashing in the spring branch, but Granma never said anything. Cherokees never scolded their children for having anything to do with the woods.

I would go far up the spring branch, wading the clear water, bending low through the green feather curtains of the weeping willows that hung down, trailing branch tips in the current. Water ferns made green lace that curved over the stream and offered holding places for the little umbrella spiders.

These little fellers would tie one end of a thin cable to the fern branch, then leap into the air, spilling out more cable in an umbrella and try to make it across to a fern branch on the other side. If he made it, he would tie the cable and jump back—back and forth—until he had a pearly looking net spread over the spring.

These were gritty little fellers. If they fell in the water, they got swept along in rapids and had to fight to stay on top and make it to the bank before a brook minnow got them.

I squatted in the middle of the spring branch and watched one little spider trying to get his cable across. He had determined that he was going to have the widest pearl net anywheres up and down the whole spring branch; and he picked a wide place. He would tie his cable, jump in the air and fall in the water. He'd get swept downstream, fighting for his life, crawl out on the bank and come back to that same fern. Then he'd try again.

The third time he come back to the fern and walked out on the end and laid down, crossing his front arms under his chin, to study the water. I figured he was might near give out—I was, and my bottom was numbing cold from squatting in the spring branch. He laid there thinking and studying. In a minute he got a thought, and commenced to jump up and down on the fern. Up and down. The fern got to rising and falling. He kept at it, jumping to move the fern down and riding it back up. Then, of a sudden, when the fern rose high, he jumped, letting out his umbrella—and he made it.

He was fired up proud and leapt around after he made it, until he nearly fell off. His pearl net become the widest I ever saw.

I got to know the spring branch, following it up the hollow: the dip swallows that hung sack nests in the willows and fussed at me until they got to know me—then they would stick out their heads and talk; the frogs that sung all along the banks, but would hush when I moved close, until Granpa told me that frogs can feel the ground shake when you walk. He showed me how the Cherokee walks, not heel down, but toe down, slipping the moccasins on the ground. Then I could come right up, and set down beside a frog and he would keep singing.

Following the spring branch was how I found the secret place. It was a little ways up the side of the mountain and hemmed in with laurel. It was not very big, a grass knoll with an old sweet gum tree bending down. When I saw it, I knew it was my secret place, and so I went there a whole lot.

Ol' Maud taken to going with me. She liked it too, and we would sit under the sweet gum and listen—and watch. Ol' Maud never made a sound in the secret place. She knew it was secret.

Once in the late afternoon me and ol' Maud was sitting with our backs against the sweet gum, and watching when

I saw a flicker of something move a ways off. It was Granma. She had passed not far from us. But I figured she hadn't seen my secret place atall or she would of said something.

Granma could move quieter than a whisper through wood leaves. I followed her and she was root gathering. I caught up to help and me and Granma set down on a log to sort the roots out. I reckined I was too young to keep a secret, for I had to tell Granma about my place. She wasn't surprised—which surprised me.

Granma said all Cherokees had a secret place. She told me she had one and Granpa had one. She said she had never asked, but she believed Granpa's was on top of the mountain, on the high trail. She said she reckined most everybody had a secret place, but she couldn't be certain, as she had never made inquiries of it. Granma said it was necessary. Which made me feel right good about having one.

Granma said everybody has two minds. One of the minds has to do with the necessaries for body living. You had to use it to figure how to get shelter and eating and such like for the body. She said you had to use it to mate and have young'uns and such. She said we had to have that mind so as we could carry on. But she said we had another mind that had nothing atall to do with such. She said it was the spirit mind.

Granma said if you used the body-living mind to think greedy or mean; if you was always cuttin' at folks with it and figuring how to material profit off'n them . . . then you would shrink up your spirit mind to a size no bigger'n a hickor'nut.

Granma said that when your body died, the body-living mind died with it, and if that's the way you had thought all your life there you was, stuck with a hickor'nut spirit, as the spirit mind was all that lived when everything else died. Then, Granma said, when you was born back—

as you was bound to be—then, there you was, born with a hickor'nut spirit mind that had practical no understanding of anything.

Then it might shrink up to the size of a pea and could disappear, if the body-living mind took over total. In such case, you lost your spirit complete.

That's how you become dead people. Granma said you could easy spot dead people. She said dead people when they looked at a woman saw nothing but dirty; when they looked at other people they saw nothing but bad; when they looked at a tree they saw nothing but lumber and profit; never beauty. Granma said they was dead people walking around.

Granma said that the spirit mind was like any other muscle. If you used it it got bigger and stronger. She said the only way it could get that way was using it to understand, but you couldn't open the door to it until you quit being greedy and such with your body mind. Then understanding commenced to take up, and the more you tried to understand, the bigger it got.

Natural, she said, understanding and love was the same thing; except folks went at it back'ards too many times, trying to pretend they loved things when they didn't understand them. Which can't be done.

I see right out that I was going to commence trying to understand practical everybody, for I sure didn't want to come up with a hickor'nut spirit.

Granma said your spirit mind could get so big and powerful that you would eventually know all about your past body lives and would get to where you could come out with no body death atall.

Granma said I could watch some of how it worked from my secret place. In the spring when everything is born (and always, when anything is born, even an idea), there's fret and fuss. There's spring storms like a baby borning in blood and pain. Granma said it was the spirits kicking up a fuss at having to get back into material forms again.

Then there was the summer—our growed-up lives—and autumn when we got older and had that peculiar feeling in our spirits of being back in time. Some folks called it nostalgia and sadness. The winter with everything dead or seeming to be, like our bodies when they die, but born again just like the spring. Granma said the Cherokees knew, and had learned it long ago.

Granma said I would come to know that the old sweet gum tree in my secret place had a spirit too. Not a spirit of humans, but a tree spirit. She said her Pa had taught her all about it.

Granma's Pa was called Brown Hawk. She said his understanding was deep. He could feel the tree-thought. Once, she said, when she was a little girl, her Pa was troubled and said the white oaks on the mountain near them was excited and scared. He spent much time on the mountain, walking among the oaks. They were of much beauty, tall and straight. They wasn't selfish, allowing ground for sumach and persimmon, and hickory and chestnut to feed the wild things. Not being selfish gave them much spirit and the spirit was strong.

Granma said her Pa got so worried about the oaks that he would walk amongst them at night, for he knew something was wrong.

Then, early one morning, as the sun broke the mountain ridge, Brown Hawk watched while lumbermen moved through the white oaks, marking and figuring how to cut all of them down. When they left, Brown Hawk said, the white oaks commenced to cry. And he could not sleep. So he watched the lumbermen. They built a road up to the mountain over which to bring their wagons.

Granma said her Pa talked to the Cherokees and they determined to save the white oaks. She said at night, when the lumbermen would leave and go back to the settlement, the Cherokees would dig up the road, hacking deep trenches across it. The women and children helped.

The next morning, the lumbermen came back and spent all day fixing the road. But that night, the Cherokees dug it up again. This went on for the next two days and nights; then the lumbermen put up guards on the road with guns. But they could not guard all the road, and the Cherokees dug trenches where they could.

Granma said it was a hard struggle and they grew very tired. Then one day, as the lumbermen were working on the road, a giant white oak fell across a wagon. It killed two mules and smashed the wagon. She said it was a fine, healthy white oak and had no reason to fall, but it did.

The lumbermen gave up trying to build the road. Spring rains set in . . . and they never came back.

Granma said the moon waxed full, and they held a celebration in the great stand of white oaks. They danced in the full yellow moon, and the white oaks sang and touched their branches together, and touched the Cherokee. Granma said they sang a death chant for the white oak who had given his life to save others, and she said the feeling was so strong that it almost picked her up off the mountain.

"Little Tree," she said, "these things you must not tell, for it will not help to tell them in this world that is the white man's. But you must know. And so I have told you."

I knew then why we only used the logs that the spirit had left for our fireplace. I knew the life of the forest . . . and the mountains.

Granma said that her Pa had such understanding that she knew he would be strong . . . where he would know, in his next body life. She said she hoped soon she would be strong too; then she would know him, and their spirits would know.

Granma said that Granpa was moving closer to the understanding without knowing it, and they would be together, always, their spirits knowing.

I asked Granma, reckin if I could get that way so I wouldn't be left behind.

She taken my hand. We walked a long way down the trail before she answered. She said for me always to try to understand. She said I would get there too, and I might even be ahead of her.

I said I didn't care a thing in the world about being ahead. It would suit me might near total if I could just catch up. It was kind of lonesome, always being left behind.

Granpa's Trade

IN ALL HIS seventy odd years, Granpa had never held a job in public works. "Public works," to mountain folks, meant *any* kind of job that paid for hire. Granpa couldn't tolerate regular hire. He said all it done was used up time without satisfaction. Which is reasonable.

In 1930, when I was five years old, a bushel of corn sold for twenty-five cents; that is, if you could find anybody that would buy a bushel of corn. Which was not likely. Even if it had sold for ten dollars a bushel, me and Granpa could not have made a living at it. Our corn patch was too little.

Granpa had a trade though. He said every man ought to have a trade and had ought to take pride in it. Granpa did. His trade was handed down on the Scotch side of his family for several hundred years. Granpa was a whiskey-maker.

When you bring up whiskey-making, most folks outside the mountains give it a bad name. But their judgments are allowed at on what big-city criminals do. Big-city criminals hire fellers to run off whiskey, not caring what kind of whiskey it is, just so they run off a lot of it—and fast. Such men will use potash or lye to "turn" their mash quick and give their whiskey a good "bead." They'll run their whiskey through sheet iron or tin and truck radiators, which has all kinds of poisons and can kill a man.

Granpa said such fellers ought to be hung. Granpa said you could make bad judgments about any trade, giving it a bad name, if you judged by the worst that was carrying on the trade.

Granpa said his clothes suit was as spankin' good as the day he married up in it, fifty-odd years ago. He said the tailor that made it had taken pride in his work; howsoever, there was tailors that didn't. Your judgment of the tailoring trade was dependent on which kind of tailor ye went by. Same as the whiskey making trade. Which is right.

Granpa would never put anything in his whiskey, not even sugar. Sugar is used to stretch out the whiskey and make more of it; but Granpa said it was not pure whiskey when this was done. He made pure whiskey; nothing but corn in the makins.

He also had no patience atall with aging whiskey. Granpa said he had heard all his life this 'un and that 'un mouthing off about how much better aged whiskey was. He said he tried it oncet. Said he set some fresh whiskey back and let it set for a week and when he tasted of it, it didn't taste one lick damn different from all the other whiskey he made.

Granpa said that where folks got that at was letting whiskey set in barrels for a long time until it picked up the scent and color of the barrels. He said if a damn fool wanted to smell of a barrel, he'd ought to go stick his head in one and smell of it, then go git hisself a drink of honest whiskey.

Granpa called such people "barrel sniffers." He said he could put stump water in a barrel and let it set long enough and sell it to such folks, and they would drink it because it smelled like a barrel.

Granpa was right put out about the whole whiskey

barrel mess. He said the thing was likely started—if it could be checked out—by big shots that could afford settin' their whiskey up for years at a time. This way they squeezed out the little man who couldn't afford to set his whiskey back to git a barrel smell. He said they spent a creekfull of money to sell their whiskey as having a better barrel smell than anybody else's, and so total fooled a lot of 'possum-headed idjits that they'd ought to drink it. But there was still sensible folks, Granpa said, who had not taken up barrel sniffin', and so the little man could still git by.

Granpa said that since whiskey-making was the only trade he knowed, and since I was five coming on to six, then he reckined I would have to learn that trade. He advised that when I got older, I might want to switch trades but I would know whiskey-making, and could always have a trade to fall back on in times when I was pushed otherwise to make a living.

I seen right off that me and Granpa had a fight on our hands with the big shots that was pushing barrel sniffin' whiskey; but I was proud that Granpa had taken me in to learn the trade.

Granpa's still was back up in the Narrows where the spring branch run out of the creek. It was set back in laurels and honeysuckle so thick that a bird couldn't find it. Granpa was proud of it, for it was pure copper; the pot and the cap arm and the coil, which was called a "worm."

It was a little still as stills go, but we didn't need a big one. Granpa only made one run a month, which always come out to eleven gallons. We sold nine gallons to Mr. Jenkins, who run the store at the crossroads, at two dollars a gallon which you can see was a lot of money for our corn.

It bought all the necessaries and put a little money back besides, and Granma kept that in a tobacco sack stuffed down in a fruit jar. Granma said that I had a share in it, for I was working hard and learning the trade too.

Our two gallons we kept there. Granpa liked to have some in his jug for occasional liquorin' and settin' in before company, and Granma used considerable of it in her cough medicine. Granpa said it was also necessary for snake bite, spider bite, heel bruises and lots of things like that.

I seen right off that stillin'—if you done it proper—was hard work.

Most people making whiskey used white corn. We didn't have any. We used Indian corn, which is the only kind we grew. It is dark red and give our whiskey a light red tint . . . which nobody else had any like. We was proud of our color. Everybody knew it when they saw it.

We would shell the corn, Granma helped, and some of it we put in a tow sack. We poured warm water over the sack and let it lay in the sun or in the winter by the fireplace. You had to turn the sack two or three times a day to keep the corn stirred up. In four or five days it had long sprouts.

The other shelled corn we ground up into meal. We couldn't stand the expense of taking it to a miller, for he would take out a toll. Granpa had built his own grist mill. It had two rocks set against each other, and we turned them with a handle.

Me and Granpa would tote the meal up the hollow and the Narrows to the still. We had a wood trough that we stuck in the spring branch and ran water to the pot 'til it was filled three quarters full. Then we poured the meal in and started a fire under the pot. We used ash wood for ash makes no smoke. Granpa said that more than likely any wood would be all right, but there was no sense in taking a chance. Which was right.

Granpa fixed me a box which we set on a stump by the pot. I stood on the box and stirred the meal water while it cooked. I couldn't see over the top and never seen exactly what I was stirring, but Granpa said I done good and was never knowed to let a batch scorch. Even when my arms got tired.

After we cooked it, we drawed it off through a slop arm in the bottom, into a barrel, and added the sprout corn which we had ground up. Then we covered the barrel and let it set. It would set for about four or five days, but each day, we had to go and stir it up. Granpa said it was "working."

After four or five days, there would be a cap of hard crust on it. We would break up the cap, until it was about gone and then we was ready to make a run.

Granpa had a big bucket and I had a little one. We dipped out the barrel and poured the beer—that's what Granpa called it—into the pot. Granpa set the cap on the pot, and we put our wood to fire under it. When the beer boiled, it sent steam up through the cap arm which was connected to the worm, the coil of copper tubing running around in circles. The worm was set in a barrel, and we had cold water from the spring branch running in our trough through the barrel. This made the steam turn back to liquid, and the worm come out at the bottom of the barrel. Where it come out, we had hickory coals to strain off the bardy grease which would make you sick if you drank it.

After all of this you would think we would get a lot of whiskey . . . but we only got about two gallons. We set the two gallons aside and drained off the "backings," which didn't turn to steam, in the pot.

Then we had to scrub the whole thing down. The two gallons we had, Granpa called them "singles." He said they was over two hundred proof. We put the backings and the singles back in the pot, started the fire, and done it all over again, adding some water. This time, we got our eleven gallons.

As I say, it was hard work and I never could figure how some folks would say that lazy, good-for-nothings made whiskey. Whoever says that without a doubt has never made any.

Granpa was the best at his trade. Whiskey can be ruined

a lot more ways than it can be made good. The fire can't be too hot. If you let the workings lay too long, vinegar sets up; if you run early, it's too weak. You must be able to read a "bead," and judge its proofing. I seen why Granpa taken such pride in his trade, and I tried to learn.

Some things I could do which Granpa said he didn't hardly see how he had managed until I come along. He would lower me into the pot after a run, and I scrubbed it out. Which I always done as fast as I could, for it was usually pretty hot. I toted ash wood and kept everything stirred up. It kept us busy.

When me and Granpa was at the still, Granma kept the dogs locked up. Granpa said if anybody was to come up the hollow, then Granma was to turn loose Blue Boy and send him up the trail. Blue Boy, having the best nose, would pick up our scent and show up at the still and then we would know somebody was on the trail.

Granpa said he started out using ol' Rippitt, but ol' Rippitt commenced eating the leftover backings and got drunk. He taken to it regular. Granpa said ol' Rippitt might near turned to steady liquorin' before he put a stop to it. Once he led ol' Maud to the still and she got drunk too. So he switched to Blue Boy.

There are many other things that a good mountain whiskey-maker must know. You have to be careful to clean up good after a run, because if you don't it will smell of sour mash. Granpa said the law was just like hound dogs and had noses fer smell that could pick up a mash scent miles away. Granpa said he reckined that this was where the name "law dogs" come from. He said if you could check it out, they was all handed down from a special bred-up line, used by kings and such, like hounds to track folks. But Granpa said if I ever had occasion to see any of them, I would notice they all had a smell about them too . . . which helped folks some in knowing they was about.

Also you had to be careful not to knock your bucket

against the pot. You can hear a bucket striking a pot for maybe two miles in the mountains. This cause me considerable worry until I got on to it, for I had to dip my bucket in the barrel, tote it to the pot, climb up on the stump and box, and lean way over to dump in the beer. I shortly got to where I never struck my bucket.

You could not sing nor whistle neither. But me and Granpa talked. Regular talk will carry a long way in the mountains. Most folks don't know—the Cherokees do— that there is a range of tone you can talk in that when it carries will sound like mountain sounds: wind in the trees and brush and maybe running water. That's the way me and Granpa talked.

We listened to the birds while we worked. If the birds fly off and the tree crickets stop singing—look out.

Granpa said there was so many things to handle in your head that I was not to worry about picking it up all at oncet; that it would come and be nature to me after a while. Which eventually it did.

Granpa had a mark for his whiskey. It was his maker's mark, scratched on top of every fruit jar lid. Granpa's mark was shaped like a tomahawk, and nobody else in the mountains used it. Each maker had his own mark. Granpa said that when he passed on, which more than likely he would eventually do, I would git the mark handed down to me. He had got it from his Pa. At Mr. Jenkins' store, there was men who come in and would not buy any other whiskey but Granpa's, with his mark.

Granpa said that as a matter of fact, since me and him was more or less partners now, half of the mark was owned by me at the present time. This was the first time I had ever owned anything, as to call it mine. So I was right proud of our mark, and seen to it, as much as Granpa, that we never turned out no bad whiskey under our mark. Which we didn't.

I guess one of the scaredest times of my life come about

while making whiskey. It was late winter, just before spring. Me and Granpa was finishing up our last run. We had sealed the half gallon fruit jars and was putting them in the tow sacks. We always put leaves in the tow sacks too, for this helped us to keep from breaking our jars.

Granpa always carried two big tow sacks with most of the whiskey. I carried a little tow sack with three half gallon jars. I eventually got to where I could carry four jars, but at that time I could only carry three. It was a pretty big load for me, and toting it back down the trail, I would have to stop considerable to set it down and rest. Granpa did too.

We was just finishing our sacking when Granpa said, "Damn! There's Blue Boy!"

There he was, laying by the side of the still with his tongue hanging out. What scared me and Granpa was that we didn't know how long he had been there. He had come up without a word and laid down. I said, "Damn!" too. (As I say, me and Granpa occasional cussed when we wasn't around Granma.)

Granpa was already listening. All the sounds was the same. The birds had not flown away. Granpa said, "Ye taken up your sack and head back down the trail. Iff'n ye see somebody, step off the trail 'til they pass. I'll take time to clean up and hide the still and go down t'other mountain side. I'll meet ye at the cabin."

I grabbed up my sack and throwed it over my shoulder so fast, it nearly jerked me over back'ards, but I wobbled out, fast as I could and got on the Narrows trail. I was scared . . . but I knew this was necessary. The still come first.

Flatlanders could never understand what it meant to bust up a mountain man's still. It would be as bad as the Chicago fire to the people in Chicago. Granpa's still had been handed down to him, and now, at his age, it was not likely that he could ever replace it. To have it busted up would not only put me and Granpa out of business, it would put me and him and Granma where it would be practical intolerable to make a living.

There was no way atall of living on twenty-five cent corn, even if you had enough corn to sell—which we didn't—and even if you could sell it—which we couldn't.

Granpa didn't have to explain to me how desperate it was that we save the still. So I taken off. It was hard to trot with the three fruit jars in my sack.

Granpa sent Blue Boy with me. I kept my eye on Blue Boy, walking just ahead of me, for he could pick a scent out of the wind long before you could hear anything.

The mountains rose high on either side of the Narrows trail, and there was just room to walk on the bank of the spring branch. Me and Blue Boy had come maybe halfway down the Narrows when we heard a big racket break out down on the hollow trail.

Granma had turned all the dogs loose and they was howling and baying up the trail. Something was wrong. I stopped and Blue Boy did too. The dogs were coming on, turning up the Narrows toward us. Blue Boy raised his ears and tail and sniffed the air; hairs ruffled on his back, and he started walking stiff-legged ahead of me. I sure appreciated ol' Blue Boy right then.

Then there they was. They come around the bend of the trail all of a sudden and stopped and looked at me. They 'peared like an army, though thinking back it was likely not more than four of them. They were the biggest fellers I had ever seen and they had badges shining on their shirts. They stood and stared at me like they had never seen such before. I stopped and watched them too. My mouth got clacker dry and my knees commenced to wobble.

"Hey!" one of them hollered, "by God . . . it's a kid!" Another one said, "A damn Indian kid!" Which, with me wearing moccasins, deer pants and shirt . . . with my hair

long and black, I couldn't hardly see no way of passing as
anything else.

One of them said, "What'cha got in that sack, kid?"
And another one hollered, "Look out for that hound!"

Blue Boy was walking real slow toward them. He was
growling low and showing his teeth. Blue Boy meant
business.

They started walking, cautious, up the trail toward me.
I seen that I could not get around them. If I jumped in the
spring branch they would catch me, and if I run back up
the trail I would be leading them to the still. That would
put me and Granpa out of business and it was my responsibility, same as Granpa's, to save the still. I taken to
the side of the mountain.

There is a way to run up a mountain; if you ever have
to run up a mountain . . . which I hope you don't. Granpa
had showed me the way Cherokees do it. You don't run
straight up, you run along the side and angle up as you
go. But you don't hardly run on the ground; this is because
you place your feet on the high side of brush and tree
trunks and roots, which gives you good footing, so you'll
never slip. You can make fast time. This is what I did.

Instead of angling up the mountain away from the
men . . . which would have taken me back up the Narrows . . . I headed up the side that led down the trail,
toward the men.

This made me pass right over their heads. They broke off
the trail toward me, thrashing in the brush, and one of
them nearly reached my foot as I passed. He did manage
to grab the brush I had stepped on and was so close I
might near knew he was going to kill me right off. But
Blue Boy bit him in the leg. He hollered and fell back'ards
on the men behind him, and I kept running.

I heard Blue Boy, he was growling and fighting. He got
kicked or hit, because I heard the wind go out of him, and
he yelped, but he was right back fighting again. I was

running all the time—fast as I could—which wasn't too fast as the fruit jars was slowing me up.

I heard the men clambering up the mountain behind me and about that time, the rest of the hounds hit. I could tell ol' Rippitt's growling and howling plain, and ol' Maud's. It all sounded pretty fearful, mixed in with the men yelling and hollering and cussing. Later on, Granpa said he heard it plumb over on the other mountain and it sounded like an entire war had broke out.

I kept running as long as I could. After a while I had to stop. I felt like I would bust; but I didn't stop long. I kept going until I was settin' right on top of the mountain. The last part of the climbing I had to drag my fruit jars, I was that wore out.

I could still hear the dogs and men. They were moving back down the Narrows trail, and then the hollow trail. It was a continuous squalling, cussing and yelling all the way; like a big ball of sound that rolled down the trail until I couldn't hear it anymore.

Though I was so tired I couldn't stand up, I felt right good about it, for they didn't go near the still, and I knew Granpa would be pleased. My legs was weak and so I laid down in the leaves and slept.

When I woke up, it was dark. The moon had come up over the far mountain, nearly full and was bringing light to the hollows, way down below me. Then I heard the hounds. I knew Granpa had sent them after me, for they didn't bay like they did on a fox trail; their voices sounded kind of whining, like they was trying to get me to answer them.

They had picked up my trail, for they were angling up the mountain. I whistled and heard them yelp and bark. In a minute, they was covering me up, licking my face and jumping all over me. Even ol' Ringer had come, and him might near blind.

Me and the hounds come down off the mountain. Ol'

Maud couldn't stand it, and run ahead barking and howling to tell Granma and Granpa I had been found. Aiming to take all the credit herself, I reckined, though she couldn't smell a lick.

As I come down the hollow I saw Granma out in the trail. She had lit the lamp and was holding it before her like she had set a light to guide me home. Granpa was with her.

They didn't come up the trail but stood and watched as I come along with the dogs. I felt good about it. I still had my fruit jars and had not broke any of them.

Granma set the lamp down and knelt to meet me. She grabbed me so hard, she nearly made me drop my fruit jars. Granpa said he would carry the fruit jars the rest of the way.

Granpa said that he couldn't have done any better hisself, and him going on seventy odd years. He said that I was likely coming on to be the finest whiskey-maker in the mountains.

Granpa said I might wind up being better'n him. Which I knew wasn't likely, but I was proud he said it.

Granma never said anything. She toted me the rest of the way home. But I could of made it, more than likely.

Trading with a Christian

THE NEXT MORNING, all the dogs was still jumping around, stiff-legged and proud. They knew they had done something which helped. I felt proud too . . . but I wasn't uppity about it, because such was part of the whiskey-making trade.

Ol' Ringer was missing. Me and Granpa whistled and hollered for him, but he didn't show up. We walked all around the cabin clearing, but he wasn't to be found anywhere. So we set off with the hounds to find him. We went up the hollow trail and the Narrows but could find no trace of him anywhere. Granpa said we had better backtrack up the mountain the way I had come down the night before. We did; first through the brush tangles, searching, and then up the mountain. Blue Boy and Little Red found him.

Ringer had run into a tree. Maybe it was the last tree he had run into, for Granpa said it looked like he had run into a lot of trees or else been hit with a club. His head was bloody all over and he lay on his side. His tongue was stabbed through with his teeth. He was alive, and Granpa picked him up in his arms and we carried him down the mountain.

We stopped at the spring branch, and me and Granpa washed the blood from his face and loosened his tongue from the teeth. There was gray hairs over his face and when I saw them I knew that ol' Ringer was very old and had no business running off in the mountains looking after me. We sat with him by the spring branch, and in a little while he opened his eyes; they were old and bleary and he could barely see.

I bent low to ol' Ringer's face and told him I 'preciated him looking for me in the mountains, and I was sorry. Ol' Ringer didn't mind, he licked my face, letting me know he'd just as soon do it all over again.

Granpa let me help carry ol' Ringer down the trail. Granpa carried most of him, but I toted his hind feet. When we got to the cabin, Granpa laid him down and said, "Ol' Ringer is dead." And he was. He had died on the trail, but Granpa said he knowed that we had come and got him, and that he was on his way home, and so he felt good about it. I felt some better too—though not much.

Granpa said ol' Ringer died like all good mountain hounds want to die: doing for their folks and in the woods.

Granpa got a shovel. We carried ol' Ringer up the hollow trail, up by the corn patch that he prided so in guarding. Granma come along too, and all the hounds followed, whining, with their tails between their legs. I felt the same.

Grandpa dug ol' Ringer's grave at the foot of a little water oak. It was a pretty place; red sumach all around in the fall, and a dogwood tree standing by with white blooms in the spring.

Granma laid a white cotton sack in the bottom of the grave, and placed ol' Ringer on it and wrapped it around him. Granpa put a big board over ol' Ringer, so the 'coons couldn't dig him up. We covered up the grave. The hounds stood around, knowing it was ol' Ringer, and ol' Maud whined. Her and ol' Ringer had been partners at the corn patch.

Granpa pulled off his hat and said, "Good-bye, ol' Ringer." I said good-bye ol' Ringer, too. And so we left him, under the water oak tree.

I felt total bad about it, and empty. Granpa said he knew how I felt, for he was feeling the same way. But Granpa said everything you lost which you had loved give you that feeling. He said the only way round it was not to love anything, which was worse because you would feel empty all the time.

Granpa said, supposin' ol' Ringer had not been faithful; then we would not be proud of him. That would be a worse feeling. Which is right. Granpa said when I got old, I would remember ol' Ringer, and I would like it—to remember. He said it was a funny thing, but when you got old and remembered them you loved, you only remembered the good, never the bad, which proved the bad didn't count nohow.

But we had to get on with our trade. Me and Granpa toted our wares over the cutoff trail to Mr. Jenkins' crossroads store. "Wares" is what Granpa called our whiskey.

I liked the cutoff trail. We went down the hollow trail, and before we reached the wagon ruts, we turned and beared left to the cutoff trail. It ran over the ridges of the mountains that sloped toward the valley like big fingers pushing out and resting in the flatlands.

The hollows we crossed were shallow between the ridges and easy to climb out of. The trail was several miles long; passing through stands of pine and cedar on the slopes; persimmon trees and honeysuckle vine.

In the fall of the year, after frost had turned the persimmons red, I would stop on the way back and fill my pockets, and then run to catch up with Granpa. In the spring, I done the same thing, picking blackberries.

Oncet, Granpa stopped and watched me pick blackberries. It was one of the times he was put out about words, and how folks was fooled by them. Granpa said, "Little Tree, did ye know that when *black*berries is *green,* they is *red?*"

This total confused me, and Granpa laughed. "The *name* is give to *black*berries . . . to describe 'em by color . . . folks use the color *green* . . . meaning they ain't ripe . . . which when they ain't ripe, they are *red.*" Which is true.

Granpa said, "That's how the damn fool word-using gits folks all twisted up. When ye hear somebody using *words* agin' somebody, don't go by his words, fer they won't make no damn sense. Go by his *tone,* and ye'll know if he's mean and lying." Granpa was pretty much down on having too many words. Which was reasonable.

There was also hickor'nuts, chinkapins, walnuts and chestnuts usually laying by the trail side. So, no matter what time of year it was, coming back from the cross-roads store kept me busy gathering.

Totin' our wares to the store was a pretty good job. I would sometimes fall far behind Granpa, carrying my three fruit jars in the sack. When I did, I knew he would be settin' down somewhere ahead, and when I got to him, we would rest.

When you toted that-a-way, by going from one settin' down place to another, it was not so hard. When we got to the last ridge, me and Granpa always set down in the bushes while we looked for the pickle barrel in front of the store. If the pickle barrel was not settin' out front that meant everything was all right. If it was settin' out front that meant the law, and we was not to deliver our wares. Everybody in the mountains watched for the pickle barrel, for other people had wares to deliver too.

I never saw the pickle barrel settin' out front, but I never failed to look for it. I had learned that the whiskey-making trade had a lot of complications to it. But Granpa said every trade has, more or less, some complications.

He said did ye ever think how it would be in the dentist trade, having to look down folks mouths all the time, day in and day out, nothing but mouths? He said such a trade would drive him total crazy and that the whiskey-making trade, with all its complications, was a sight better trade for a feller to be in. Which is right.

I like Mr. Jenkins. He was big and fat and wore overalls. He had a white beard that hung down over the bib of his overalls, but his head was near totally without hair; it shined like a pine knob.

He had all kinds of things in the store: big racks of shirts and overalls and boxes of shoes. There was barrels with crackers in them, and on a counter he had a big hoop of cheese. Also on the counter he had a glass case which had candy laid on the shelves. There was all kinds of candy and looked like there was more candy than he could ever run out of. I never seen anybody eat any of it, but I guess he sold some or he wouldn't have had it.

Every time we delivered our wares, Mr. Jenkins asked me if I would go to his woodpile and pick up a sack of wood chips for the big stove that set in the store. I always did. The first time, he offered me a big stick of striped candy, but I couldn't rightly take it just for picking up wood chips, which wasn't hardly no trouble atall. He put it back in the case, and found another piece which was old and which he was going to throw away. Granpa said that it was all right for me to take it, seeing as how Mr. Jenkins was going to throw it away, and it would not be of benefit to anybody. So I did.

Every month, he come across another old stick, and I guess I might near cleaned out his old candy. Which he said helped him out a lot.

It was at the crossroads store where I got slickered out of my fifty cents. It had taken me a long time to accumulate the fifty cents. Granma would put aside a nickel or dime in a jar for me each month we delivered our wares.

It was my part of the trade. I liked to carry it, all in nickels and dimes, in my pocket when we went to the crossroads store. I never spent it and each time when we got home I put it back in the fruit jar.

It was a comfort to me, carrying it in my pocket to the store, and knowing it was mine. I kind of had my eye on a big red and green box which was in the candy case. I didn't know how much it cost, but I was figuring that maybe next Christmas I would buy it for Granma . . . and then we would eat what was in it. But as I say, I got slickered out of my fifty cents before then.

It was about dinnertime of a day right after we had delivered our wares. The sun was straight overhead and me and Granpa was resting, squattin' down under the store shed with our backs against the store. Granpa had bought some sugar for Granma and three oranges which Mr. Jenkins had. Granma liked oranges, which I did too, when you could get them. Seeing Granpa had three, I knew I would get one.

I was eating on my stick candy. Men commenced to come to the store in twos and threes. They said a politician was coming and was going to make a speech. I don't know that Granpa would have stayed, for as I say he didn't give a lick damn about politicians, but before we got rested here come the politician.

He was in a big car, kicking up rolls of dust from the road, so everybody saw him a long way off before he got there. He had some feller driving his car for him, and he got out of the back seat. There was a lady in the back seat with him. All the time the politician talked, she throwed out little cigarettes that she had smoked part of. Granpa said they were ready-roll, tailor-made cigarettes, which rich people smoked as they was too lazy to roll their own.

The politician come around and shook everybody's hand; though he didn't shake mine nor Granpa's. Granpa said this was because we looked like Indians and didn't vote nohow, so we was of practical no use whatsoever to the politician. Which sounds reasonable.

He wore a black coat and had a white shirt with a ribbon tied at his neck; it was black and hung down. He laughed a lot and 'peared to be mighty happy. That is, until he got mad.

He got up on a box and commenced to get worked up about conditions in Washington City . . . which he said was total going to hell. He said it wasn't a thing in the world but Sodom and Gomorrah, which I guess it was. He got madder and madder about it and untied the ribbon around his neck.

He said the Catholics was behind every damn bit of it. He said they was practical in control of the whole thing, and was aiming to put Mr. Pope in the White House. Catholics, he said, was the rottenest, low-downest snakes that ever lived. He said they had fellers called priests that mated women called nuns, and the young'uns that come of the matin', they fed them to a pack of dogs. He said it was the awfulest thing he had ever seen nor heard tell of. Which it was.

He got to hollerin' pretty loud about it, and I guess, conditions being what they was in Washington City, it was enough to make a man holler. He said if it wasn't for him puttin' up a fight agin' them, that they would be in total control and spread plumb down to where we was at . . . which sounded pretty bad.

He said if they did, they would put all the womenfolks in convents and such . . . and would practical wipe out the young'uns. There didn't seem hardly any way atall to whip them unless everybody sent him to Washington City to see that it was done; and he said even then it would be a hard fight, because fellers was selling out to them all over the place, for money. He said he wouldn't take no money, as he had no use for it, and was total agin' it.

He said he felt like might near giving up sometimes and quittin' and just takin' it easy, like we done.

I felt right bad, takin' it easy; but when he finished talking, he got down from the box and commenced to laugh and shake hands with everybody. Which it looked like he had plenty of confidence he could handle the situation in Washington City.

I felt a little better about it, dependent on his gittin' back up there so he could whip the Catholics and such.

While he was shaking hands and talking to folks, a feller walked up to the fringe of the crowd leading a little brown calf on a rope.

He stood around watching the crowd and shook hands twicet with the politician, each time he come by. The little calf stood spraddle-legged behind him with its head down. I got up and edged over to the calf. I petted it oncet, but it wouldn't lift its head. The feller looked down at me from under a big hat. He had sharp eyes that crinkled nearly shut when he smiled. He smiled.

"Like my calf, boy?"

"Yes, sir," I said, and stepped back from the calf, as I didn't want him to think I was bothering it.

"Go ahead," he said, real cheerful. "Go ahead and pet the calf. Ye won't hurt 'em." I petted the calf.

The feller spit tobacco juice over the calf's back. "I can see," he said, "that my calf takes to ye . . . more'n anybody he's ever taken up with . . . seems like he wants to go with ye." I couldn't tell that the calf looked the way he said, but it was his calf, and he ought to know. The feller knelt down in front of me, "Have you got any money, boy?"

"Yes, sir," I said, "I got fifty cents." The feller frowned, and I could see it wasn't much money and was sorry that it was all I had.

He smiled after a minute and said, "Well, this here calf is worth more'n a hundred times that much." I seen right off it worth that much. "Yes, sir," I said, "I wasn't figuring no way atall to buy it." The feller frowned again, "Well," he said, "I'm a Christian man. Somehow or 'nother, even costing me all that this here calf is worth, I feel in my heart ye'd ought to have it, the way it's taken up with ye." He thought on this for a while, and I could see right off that it pained him a lot to think of parting with the calf.

"I ain't—ner wouldn't take him atall, mister," I said.

But the feller held up his hand to stop me. He sighed, "I'm a'goin' to let ye have the calf, son, fer fifty cents fer I feel it's my Christian duty, and—no—I won't take no fer an answer. Jest give me yer fifty cents, and the calf is your'n."

Since he put it that-a-way, I couldn't hardly turn him down. I taken out all my nickels and dimes and give them to him. He passed the calf's rope to me, and walked off so quick, I didn't know which way he went.

But I felt mighty proud of my calf, even though I had more or less taken advantage of the feller—him being a Christian, which, as he said, handicapped him somewhat. I pulled my calf around to Granpa and showed it to him. Granpa didn't seem as proud of my calf as I was, but I reckined it was because it was mine, and not his. I told him he could have half of it, seeing as how we was practically partners in the whiskey-making trade. But Granpa just grunted.

The crowd was breaking up around the politician, everybody being more or less agreed that the politician had better git to Washington City right off and fight the Catholics. He passed out pieces of paper. Though he didn't give me one, I got one off the ground. It had his picture on it, showing him smiling like there wasn't a thing wrong in Washington City. He looked real young in the picture.

Granpa said we was ready to set out for home, so I put the politician's picture in my pocket, and led my calf behind Granpa. It was pretty hard going. My calf couldn't hardly walk. It stumbled and wobbled along, and I pulled on the rope best I could. I was afraid if I pulled too hard, my calf would fall down.

I was beginning to worry if I would ever get it to the cabin, and that maybe it was sick . . . even though it was worth a hundred times what I paid for it.

By the time I got to the top of the first ridge, Granpa was nearly at the bottom fixing to head across a hollow. I seen I would be left behind, so I yelled, "Granpa . . . do ye know any Catholics?" Granpa stopped. I pulled harder on my calf and commenced to catch up. Granpa waited until me and the calf come up to him.

"I seen one, oncet," Granpa said, "at the county seat." Me and the calf caught up, and was resting as hard as we could. "One I seen," Granpa said, "didn't look particular mean . . . though I figgered he had been in some kind of scrape . . . he had got his collar twisted up, and more than likely was jest drunk enough that he failed to notice it. He 'peared to be, howsoever, peaceful enough."

Granpa set down on a rock, and I seen he was going to give some thought to it, for which I was glad. My calf had his front legs spraddled in front of him and was pantin' pretty hard.

"Howsoever," Granpa said, "iff'n ye taken a knife and cut fer half a day into that politician's gizzard, ye'd have a hard time finding a kernel of truth. Ye'll notice the son of a bitch didn't say a thing about gittin' the whiskey tax taken off . . . 'er the price of corn . . . 'er nothin' else fer that matter." Which was right.

I told Granpa that I had noticed the son of a bitch never said a word about it.

Granpa reminded me that "son of a bitch" was a new cuss word, and was not to be used no way atall around Granma. Granpa said he didn't give a lick damn if priests and nuns mated every day in the week, no more'n he cared how many bucks and does mated. He said that was their matin' business.

Granpa said that as far as them feedin' young'uns to dogs, that there would never come a day when a doe would feed her young to a dog, ner a woman, so he knowed that was a lie. Which is right.

I commenced to feel some better about the Catholics. Granpa said that wasn't no doubt in his mind that the Catholics would like to git control . . . but he said, iff'n ye had a hog and ye didn't want it stole, jest git ten or twelve men to guard it, each one of which wanted to steal it. He said that hog would be safe as in yer own kitchen. Granpa said they was all so crooked in Washington City, that they had to watch one another all the time.

Granpa said that they was so many trying to git control, it was a continual dogfight all the time anyhow. He said the worst thing wrong with Washington City was it had so many damn politicians in it.

Granpa said, that even being that we went to a hard-shell Baptist church, he would sure hate to see the hard-shells git control. He said they was total agin' liquor drinking except maybe some fer theirselves. He said they would dry the whole country up.

I seen right off there was other dangers besides the Catholics. If the hard-shells got control, me and Granpa would be put out of the whiskey-making trade, and would likely starve to death.

I asked Granpa if it wasn't likely that the big shots, which made barrel sniffin' whiskey, wasn't trying to git control too; us putting a dent in their trade and all, so they could put us out of business. Granpa said that without a doubt they was trying hard as they could, bribing politicians practical every day in Washington City.

Granpa said they was only one thing certain. The Indian was not never going to git control. Which appeared not likely.

While Granpa was talking my calf laid down and died. He just laid over on his side and there he was. I was standing in front of Granpa holding onto the rope, and Granpa pointed behind me and said, "Yer calf is dead." He never owned to half of it being his.

I got down on my knees and tried to prop its head up and get it on its feet, but it was limp. Granpa shook his head, "It's dead, Little Tree. When something is dead . . . it's dead." Which it was. I squatted by my calf and looked at it. It was might near close to being as bad a time as I could remember. My fifty cents was gone, and the red and green box of candy. And now my calf—being worth a hundred times what I paid for it.

Granpa pulled his long knife from his moccasin boot and cut the calf open and pulled out its liver. He pointed at the liver. "It's speckled and diseased. We can't eat it."

It looked to me like there wasn't anything atall that could be done with it. I didn't cry—but I might near did. Granpa knelt and skinned the calf. "Reckin Granma would give ye a dime fer the skin; likely she can use it," he said. "And we'll send the dogs back . . . they can eat the calf." Reckin that was all that could be made of it. I followed Granpa down the trail—carrying the hide of my calf— all the way to the cabin.

Granma didn't ask me, but I told her I couldn't put my fifty cents back in the jar, for I had spent it for a calf— which I didn't have. Granma give me a dime for the hide and I put that in the jar.

It was hard to eat that night, though I liked ground peas and corn bread.

While we was eating, Granpa looked at me and said, "Ye see, Little Tree, ain't no way of learning, except by letting ye do. Iff'n I had stopped ye from buying the calf, ye'd have always thought ye'd ought to had it. Iff'n I'd told ye to buy it, ye'd blame me fer the calf dying. Ye'll have to learn as ye go."

"Yes, sir," I said.

"Now," Granpa said, "what did ye learn?"

"Well," I said, "I reckin I learned not to trade with Christians."

Granma commenced to laugh. I didn't see hardly anything funny atall about it. Granpa looked dumbstruck; then he laughed so hard he choked on his corn bread. I figgered I had learned something funny but I didn't know what it was.

Granma said, "What ye mean, Little Tree, is that ye'll be likely to have caution at the next feller who tells you how good and what a fine feller he is."

"Yes, ma'am," I said, "I reckin."

I wasn't sure about anything . . . except I had lost my fifty cents. Being plumb wore out, I went to sleep at the table and my head come down in my supper plate. Granma had to wash ground peas off my face.

That night I dreamed the hard-shells and Catholics come amongst us. The hard-shells tore up our still, and the Catholics et up my calf.

A big Christian was there, smiling at the whole thing. He had a red and green box of candy and said it was worth a hundred times as much, but I could have it for fifty cents. Which I didn't have—fifty cents; and so could not buy it.

At the Crossroads Store

GRANMA TAKEN a pencil and paper and showed me how much I had lost on my trade with the Christian. Turns out, I didn't lose but forty cents, as I cleared a dime off the calf hide. I put the dime in my fruit jar and didn't take it in my pocket no more, it being safer in the jar.

On our next run I made a dime, and Granma upped it with a nickel. This give me twenty-five cents, so I was beginning to get my money built back up.

Though I had lost fifty cents at the store, I always looked forward to delivering our wares; though carrying my tow sack was a pretty good job.

I was learning five words a week out of the dictionary, and Granma would explain the meanings, then had me put the words in sentences. I used my sentences considerable on the way to the store. This would get Granpa to stop while he figured out what I was saying. I could catch up and rest with my fruit jars. Sometimes Granpa would totally knock out words, saying I didn't have to use that word no more, which speeded me up considerable in the dictionary.

Like the time I had got down to the word "abhor."

Granpa had got way ahead of me on the trail, and I had been practicing a sentence with that word so I hollered to Granpa, "I *abhor* briers, yeller jackets and such."

Granpa stopped. He waited until I had caught up with him, and set down my load of fruit jars. "What did ye say?" Granpa asked.

"I said, I *abhor* briers, yeller jackets and such," I said. Granpa looked down at me so steady-hard that I commenced to feel uneasy about the whole thing. "What in hell," Granpa said, "has whores got to do with briers and yeller jackets?"

I told him that I didn't have no way in the world of knowing, which I didn't, but the word was "*ab*hor" and it meant that you couldn't hardly stand something.

Granpa said, "Well, why don't ye just say ye can't stand it, instead of using 'ab*whore*'?" I said I couldn't figure that out myself but it was in the dictionary. Granpa got pretty worked up about it. He said the meddlesome son of a bitch that invented the dictionary ought to be taken out and shot.

Granpa said that more'n likely this same feller had worked up half a dozen more words that could discolor the meaning of the same thing. He said this was why politicians could git away with slicker'n folks and always claiming they didn't say this 'er that—or that they did. Granpa said, if you could check it out, the damn dictionary was either put up by a politician or they was some behind it. Which sounds reasonable.

Granpa said I could just knock out that word. Which I did. There was usually a lot of men around the store in the winter time or during laying-by time. "Laying-by" time was usually in August. That was the time of year after the farmers had done with plowing and hoeing weeds out of their crops four or five times; and the crops was big enough now that they "laid by," that is, no hoeing or plowing, while the crops ripened and they waited to do the gathering.

After we delivered our wares, and Granpa got paid, and I had picked up the wood chips for Mr. Jenkins and taken the stick of old candy off his hands, me and Granpa always squatted under the store shed with our backs against the wall and kind of stretched out the time.

Granpa had eighteen dollars in his pocket . . . of which I would get at least a dime when we got home. He had usually bought sugar or coffee for Granma . . . sometimes, a little wheat flour, if things was going good. Besides, we had just finished up a pretty hard week in the whiskey-making trade.

I always finished off the stick of old candy while we set. It was a good time.

We listened to the men talking about things. Some of them said there was a depression and fellers was jumping out of winders in New York and shootin' theirselves in the head about it. Granpa never said anything. Which I didn't either. But Granpa told me that New York was crowded all up with people who didn't have enough land to live on, and likely half of them was run crazy from living that-a-way, which accounted for the shootin's and the winder jumping.

Usual, there was somebody cuttin' hair at the store. They would set a straight chair under the shed and take turns gettin' their hair sheared by a feller.

Another man—everybody called him "Old Man Barnett" --jumped teeth. Not many people could "jump teeth." This was when you had a bad tooth and had to get it taken out.

Everybody liked to watch Old Man Barnett working, jumping teeth. He would set the feller whose tooth he was going to jump down in a chair. Then he would heat up a wire over a fire until the wire was red hot. He stuck the wire on the tooth and then taken a nail and placed it against the tooth, and with a hammer, he hit it a secret way. The tooth just jumped out on the ground. He was right proud of his trade, and would make everybody stand back while he done it so they wouldn't nobody learn it.

One time, another old feller about the same age as Old Man Barnett—they called him Mr. Lett—he come to get a bad tooth jumped. Old Man Barnett set Mr. Lett down in the chair and heated up his wire. He stuck the wire to Mr. Lett's tooth, but Mr. Lett wrapped his tongue around the wire. He bellered louder'n a bull and kicked Old Man Barnett in the stomach, knocking him over backwards.

This made Old Man Barnett mad and he hit Mr. Lett in the head with a chair. They got to fighting on the ground until everybody crowded in and pulled them apart. They stood cussing one another awhile—or leastwise Old Man Barnett was cussing—you couldn't understand what Mr. Lett was saying, but he was mad!

Finally they calmed down and a bunch of men held Mr. Lett and drawed out his tongue and poured turpentine on it. He left. It was the first time I ever saw Old Man Barnett fail to jump a tooth, and he didn't take it lightly. He taken pride in his trade and went around explaining to everybody why it was that he hadn't jumped that tooth. He said it was Mr. Lett's fault. Which I reckin it was.

I made up my mind right then that I was not ever going to have a bad tooth. Or if I did, I wasn't going to tell Old Man Barnett about it.

At the store is where I got acquainted with the little girl. She would come with her Pa during laying-by time, or in the winter. Her Pa was a young man who wore ragged overalls and was, most time, barefooted. The little girl was always barefooted, even when it was cold.

Granpa said they was sharecroppers. He said share-croppers didn't own no land, or nothing else to speak of—usually not even a bedstead or a chair. They would work on somebody else's land and would sometimes get half of what the owner got for his crop, but mostly they just got a third. They called it working on "halves," or on "thirds."

Granpa said by the time everything was taken out, what

they had et all year, and the seed and fertilizer cost—which the landlord paid for—and use of mules, and about everything else, it always turned up that the sharecropper didn't actual make nothing but something to eat. And not much of that.

Granpa said the bigger family that a sharecropper had, the better chance he had of gittin' on with a landlord, for then everybody in the family worked in the fields. A big family could do more work. He said sharecroppers all tried to have big families, for it was necessary. He said the wives worked in the fields, pickin' cotton and hoeing and such, and put their babies under shade trees or somewheres to scuffle for theirselves.

Granpa said Indians would not do it. He said he would take to the woods and run rabbits fer a living before he'd do it. But he said somehow or another some folks got caught in it and couldn't git out.

Granpa said it was the fault of the damn politicians who spent all their time yammerin' around using up words instead of working at the trade they was supposed to work at. He said some landlords was mean and some wasn't, like everybody else, but it always come out at "settlin' up" time, after the crops was gathered, that more'n likely there was a big disappointment.

That's why sharecroppers moved every year. Every winter they would hunt for a new landlord and find one. They would move to another shack, and set around the kitchen table at night, the Pa and Ma, and build up dreams as to how *this* year on *this* place they was going to make it.

Granpa said they held on to that all during spring and summer until the crops was gathered, then it was all bitter again. That's why they moved every year, and folks that didn't understand, called them "shiftless," which Granpa said was another damn word, like calling them "irresponsible," fer having so many young'uns—which they had to do.

Me and Granpa talked about it on the trail home and he got so worked up about it that we rested might near an hour.

I got worked up about it too, and seen right off that Granpa had a total understanding of politicians. I told Granpa that the sons of bitches ought to be run off. Granpa stopped talking about it, and cautioned me again that "son of a bitch" was brand-new cuss words that carried much starch and that Granma would total put us out of the cabin if I used them around her. I marked that down right then. It was a pretty powerful set of words.

The little girl come and stood in front of me one day while I was squattin' under the store shed eating the old candy. The little girl's Pa was in the store. She had tangled-up hair and her teeth was rotten; I hoped Old Man Barnett didn't see her. She wore a tow sack for a dress and just stood looking at me, and crossing her toes back and forth in the dirt. I felt right bad, eating the candy, and so I told her she could lick on it for a while, if she didn't bite off any, for I would have to have it back. She took the candy and licked on it pretty regular.

She said she could pick a hundred pounds of cotton in a day. She said she had a brother that could pick two hundred pounds and that her Ma—when she was feeling right—could pick three hundred. She said she had knowed her Pa to pick five hundred pounds if he picked into the nighttime.

She said they didn't put rocks in their pickin' sacks neither, to cheat on the weight, and was knowed for giving a honest day's work. She said her whole and entire family was knowed for that.

She asked me how much cotton I could pick, and I told her I had never picked none. She said she figgered that; for everybody knowed that Indians was lazy and wouldn't work. I taken back my candy. But she said, after that, that it wasn't because we could help it—that we was just different and maybe we done other things. I let her lick some more on the candy.

It was still wintertime, and she said their family was all listening for the turtledove. It was well knowed, she said, that whatever direction you heard the turtledove calling, that was the direction you was going to move the next year.

She said they had not heard it yet, but was expecting to just anytime, for they had been total cheated by the landlord, and her Pa had fell out with him so they had to move. She said her Pa had come to the store to see about talking to somebody there that might want a good family on their place which was knowed for giving honest work and causing no trouble atall. She said she expected they would come up with about the best place they could have ever thought of, for her Pa said the word was gittin' around about what hard workers they was, and so next year they would be settin' pretty.

She said that after the crops was in on the new place they would be going to, she was going to git a doll. She said her Ma said it would be a store-bought doll that had real hair and eyes that would open and close. She said more than likely she would git a whole lot of other things too, as they would be practical rich.

I told her we didn't own no land, except the mountain hollow with our corn patch, and that we was mountain folk with no use atall for valley farming and flatlands. I told her I had a dime.

She wanted to see it, but I told her it was at home in a fruit jar. I said I didn't carry it because a Christian had slickered me out of fifty cents oncet, and I was no wise figuring for another'n to slicker me out of my dime.

She said she was a Christian. She said she got the Holy Ghost oncet at a bush arbor meetin' and got saved. She said her Pa and Ma got the Holy Ghost practical every time they went and said they would talk in the unknown tongue when they got it. She said being a Christian made you happy and that bush arbors was times when they was happiest, being full of the Holy Ghost and all. She said I was going to hell as I hadn't been saved.

I seen right off she was a Christian, for while she was talking, she had licked my stick candy down to practical a nub. I got back what was left of it.

I told Granma about the little girl. Granma made a pair of moccasin slippers. The top part of the moccasins she made with some of my calf hide, leaving the hair on. They were pretty. Granma put two little red colored beads on the top of each moccasin.

Next month, when we went to the store, I give the moccasins to the little girl and she put them on. I told her Granma made them for her, and they didn't cost nothing. She run up and down in front of the store, watching her feet, and you could tell she was proud of the moccasins for she would stop and run her fingers over the red beads. I told her the hair hide come from my calf, which I had sold to Granma.

When her Pa come out of the store, she followed him down the road, skipping in her moccasins. Me and Granpa watched them. When they got a little ways down the road, the man stopped and looked at the little girl. He talked to her, and she pointed back towards me.

The man went to the side of the road and cut a keen switch from a persimmon bush. He held the little girl by one arm and whipped her on the legs, hard, and on the back. She cried, but she didn't move. He whipped her until the switch wore out . . . and everybody under the store shed watched . . . but they didn't say anything.

Then he made the little girl set down in the road and pull off the moccasins. He come walking back, holding the moccasins in his hand, and me and Granpa stood up. He didn't pay any attention to Granpa, but walked right up and looked down at me, and his face was hard and his eyes shining. He poked the moccasins at me—which I taken—and he said, "We'uns don't take no charity . . . from nobody . . . and especial heathen savages!"

I was right scared. He whirled around and walked off down the road, his ragged overalls flapping. He walked right by the little girl, and she followed him. She wasn't crying. She walked stiff with her head up real proud and didn't turn to look at anybody. You could see the big red stripes on her legs. Me and Granpa left.

On the trail, Granpa said he didn't bear the sharecropper no ill. Granpa said he reckined that pride was all he had . . . howsoever misplaced. He said the feller figgered he couldn't let the little girl, ner any of his young'uns, come to love pretty things for they couldn't have them. So he whipped them when they showed a liking for things they couldn't have . . . and he whipped them until they learned; so that in a little while, they knowed they was not to expect them things.

They could look forward to the Holy Ghost as gittin' their happy times, and they had their pride—and next year.

Granpa said he didn't fault me fer not catching on right off. He said he had the advantage, fer years ago, as he walked a trail near a sharecropper's shack, he had seen a feller come out in his backyard where two of his little girls was looking, settin' under a shade tree, at a Sears Roebuck catalog.

Granpa said that feller took a switch and whipped them young'uns 'till the blood run out of their legs. He said he watched, and the feller took the Sears Roebuck catalog and he went out behind the barn. He burned up the catalog, tore it all up first, like he hated that catalog. Granpa said then the feller set down against the barn, where nobody could see him, and he cried. Granpa said he seen that and so he knowed.

Granpa said ye had to understand. But most people

didn't want to—it was too much trouble—so they used words to cover their own laziness and called other folks "shiftless."

I toted the moccasin slippers home. I put them under my tow sack where I kept my overalls and shirt. I didn't look at them; they reminded me of the little girl.

She never come back to the crossroads store, ner her Pa. So I reckin they moved.

I figgered they heard the turtledove from far away.

A Dangerous Adventure

INDIAN VIOLETS come first in the mountain springtime. Just about when you figure there won't be a spring, there they are. Icy blue as the March wind, they lie against the ground, so tiny that you'll miss them unless you look close and sure.

We picked them there on the mountainside. I helped Granma, until our fingers would get numb in the raw wind. Granma made a tonic tea from them. She said I was a fast picker. Which I was.

On the high trail, where the ice still crunched beneath our moccasins, we got evergreen needles. Granma put them in hot water and we drank that too. It is better for you than any fruit, and makes you feel good. Also the roots and seeds of skunk cabbage.

Once I learned how, I was the best at acorn gathering. At first I would take each acorn as I found it to Granma's sack; but she pointed out that I could wait until I got a handful before I run to the sack. It was easy for me, being close to the ground, so that I soon was able to get more acorns in the sack than Granma.

She ground them up into a meal that was yellow-gold,

and mixed hickor'nuts and walnuts in the meal and made bread fritters; which there has never been anything to taste like.

Sometimes she had an accident in the kitchen and spilled sugar in the acorn meal. She would say, "Dum me, Little Tree. I spilt sugar in the acorn meal." I never said anything but when she did that I always got an extra fritter.

Me and Granpa was both pretty heavy acorn fritter eaters.

Then sometime there in late March, after the Indian violets had come, we would be gathering on the mountain and the wind, raw and mean, would change for just a second. It would touch your face as soft as a feather. It had an earth smell. You knew springtime was on the way.

The next day, or the next (you would commence to hold your face out for the feel), the soft touch would come again. It would last a little longer and be sweeter and smell stronger.

Ice would break and melt on the high ridges, swelling the ground and running little fingers of water down into the spring branch.

Then the yellow dandelions poked up everywhere along the lower hollow, and we picked them for greens—which are good when you mix them with fireweed greens, poke salat and nettles. Nettles make the best greens, but have little tiny hairs on them that sting you all over when you're picking. Me and Granpa many times failed to notice a nettle patch, but Granma would find it and we would pick them. Granpa said he had never knowed anything in life that, being pleasurable, didn't have a damn catch to it—somewheres. Which is right.

Fireweed has a big purple flower on it. It has a long stalk which you can peel and eat raw, or you can cook it and it is like asparagus.

Mustard comes through on the mountainside in patches that look like yellow blankets. It grows little bright canary heads with peppery leaves. Granma mixed it with other greens and sometimes ground the seeds into paste and made a table mustard.

Everything growing wild is a hundred times stronger than tame things. We pulled the wild onions from the ground and just a handful would carry more flavor than a bushel of tame onions.

As the air warms, and rains come, the mountain flowers pop colors out like paint buckets have been spilled all over the mountainsides. Firecracker flowers have long, rounded, red blooms that are so bright they look like painted paper; the harebell pushes little bluebells, dangling on stems as fine as vines, from amongst rocks and crevices. Bitterroot has big lavender-pink faces with yellow centers that hug the ground, while moonflowers are hidden deep in the hollow, long-stemmed and swaying like willows with pink-red fringes on top.

Different kinds of seed are born at different body heats in Mon-a-lah's womb. When She first begins warming, only the tiniest flowers come through. But as She warms more, bigger flowers are born, and the sap starts running up in the trees, making them swell like a woman at birthing time until they pop open their buds.

When the air gets heavy so it's hard to breathe, you know what's coming. The birds come down from the ridges and hide in the hollows and in the pines. Heavy black clouds float over the mountain, and you run for the cabin.

From the cabin porch we would watch the big bars of light that stand for a full second, maybe two, on the mountaintop, running out feelers or lightning wire in all directions before they're jerked back into the sky. Cracking claps of sound, so sharp you know something has split wide open—then the thunder rolls and rumbles over the ridges and back through the hollows. I was pretty near sure, a time or two, that the mountains was falling down, but Granpa said they wasn't. Which of course, they didn't.

Then it comes again—and rolls blue fireballs off rocks on the ridge tops and splatters the blue in the air. The trees whip and bend in the sudden rushes of wind, and the sweep of heavy rain comes thunking from the clouds in big drops, letting you know there's some real frog-strangling sheets of water coming close behind.

Folks who laugh and say that all is known about Nature, and that Nature don't have a soul-spirit, have never been in a mountain spring storm. When She's birthing spring, She gets right down to it, tearing at the mountains like a birthing woman clawing at the bed quilts.

If a tree has been hanging on, having weathered all the winter winds, and She figures it needs cleaning out, She whips it up out of the ground and flings it down the mountain. She goes over the branches of every bush and tree, and after She feels around a little with Her wind fingers, then She whips them clean and proper of anything that is weak.

If She figures a tree needs removing and won't come down from the wind, She just *whams!* and all that's left is a torch blazing from a lightning stroke. She's alive and paining. You'll believe it too.

Granpa said She was—amongst other things—tidying up any afterbirth that might be left over from last year; so Her new birthing would be clean and strong.

When the storm is over, the new growth, tiny and light, timid-green, starts edging out on the bushes and tree limbs. Then Nature brings April rain. It whispers down soft and lonesome, making mists in the hollows and on the trails where you walk under the drippings from hanging branches of trees.

It is a good feeling, exciting—but sad too—in April rain. Granpa said he always got that kind of mixed-up feeling. He said it was exciting because something new was being born, and it was sad, because you knowed you can't hold onto it. It will pass too quick.

April wind is soft and warm as a baby's crib. It

breathes on the crab apple tree until white blossoms open out, smeared with pink. The smell is sweeter than honeysuckle and brings bees swarming over the blossoms. Mountain laurel with pink-white blooms and purple centers grow everywhere, from the hollows to the top of the mountain, alongside of the dogtooth violet that has long, pointed yellow petals with a white tooth hanging out (they always looked to me like tongues).

Then, when April gets its warmest, all of a sudden the cold hits you. It stays cold for four or five days. This is to make the blackberries bloom and is called "blackberry winter." The blackberries will not bloom without it. That's why some years there are no blackberries. When it ends, that's when the dogwoods bloom out like snowballs over the mountainside in places you never suspicioned they grew: in a pine grove or stand of oak of a sudden there's a big burst of white.

The white farmers gathered out of their gardens in late summer, but the Indian gathers from early spring, when the first greens start growing, all through the summer and fall, gathering acorns and nuts. Granpa said the woods would feed you, if you lived with the woods, instead of tearing them up.

However, there is a right smart bit of work to it. I figured I was more than likely best at berry picking, for I could get in the middle of a berry patch and never have to bend down to reach the berries. I never got much tired of picking berries.

There were dewberries, blackberries, elderberries, which Granpa said makes the best wine, huckleberries and the red bearberries, which I could never find had any taste to them, but Granma used them in cooking. I always brought back more red bearberries in my bucket as they were not good to eat, and I et berries fairly regular while I was picking them. Granpa did too. But he said it wasn't like he was wasting them, because we would eventually eat them anyway. Which was right. Poke salat berries, however, are poison and they will knock you deader than last year's corn stalk. Any berries you see the birds don't eat, you had better not eat.

During berry picking time, my teeth, tongue and mouth was a pretty continual deep blue color. When me and Granpa delivered our wares, some flatlanders around the crossroads store remarked that I was sick. Occasional a new flatlander would get worked up about it when he saw me. Granpa said they showed their ignorance of what a berry picker had to put up with and I wasn't to pay any attention to them. Which I didn't.

The birds had a trick about wild cherries. Along about July, the sun would have been on the cherries just enough.

Sometimes, in the lazy sun of summer, after dinnertime, when Granma would be napping, me and Granpa would be setting on the back door stoop. Granpa would say. "Let's go up the trail, and see what we can find." Up the trail we would go, and set down in the shade of a cherry tree with our backs to the trunk. We would watch the birds.

One time we watched a thrush turn flips on a limb and wobble out to the end, like he was walking a tightrope, and then he walked plumb off the end. A robin got to feeling so good, that he wobbled right up to me and Granpa and lit up on Granpa's knee. He fussed at Granpa and told him what he thought about the whole thing. He eventually decided he would sing, but his voice squeaked and he give it up. He staggered off into the brush, with me and Granpa practical laughing ourselves sick. Granpa said he laughed so hard it hurt his gizzard. Which it did mine too.

We saw a red cardinal eat so many cherries that he keeled over and passed out on the ground. We put him in the crotch of a tree so he wouldn't get killed by something during the night.

Early the next morning me and Granpa went back to

the tree and there he was, still sleeping. Granpa punched him awake, and he got up feeling mean. He flew down at Granpa's head a time or two, and Granpa had to slap at him with his hat to make him go on. He flew down to the spring branch and stuck his head in the water and taken it out . . . and puffed and spewed and looked around like he was personally going to whip the first thing he saw.

Granpa said he believed that ol' cardinal held me and him personally responsible for his condition, though Granpa said he ought to know better. Granpa said he had seen him before—he was an old-time cherry eater.

Every bird that comes around your cabin in the mountains is a sign of something. That's what the mountain folks believe, and if you want to believe you can, for it's so. I believed. So did Granpa.

Granpa knew all the bird signs. It is good luck to have a house wren live in your cabin. Granma had a little square cut out of the top corner in the kitchen door, and our house wren flew in and out, building her nest on the eave log over the kitchen stove. She nested there, and her mate would come and feed her.

House wrens like to be around people who love birds. She would cozy down in her nest and watch us in the kitchen with little black bead eyes that shined in the lamplight. When I would drag a chair close and stand on it, so I could get a better look, she would fuss at me; but she wouldn't leave her nest.

Granpa said she loved to fuss at me. It proved to her that she was more than likely more important in the family than I was.

Whippoorwills start singing at dusk. They get their name from their call for that is what they say: *whip*-or-*will*, over and over. If you light the lamp, they will move closer and closer to the cabin and will eventually sing you to sleep. They are a sign of night peace and good dreams, Granpa said.

The screech owl hollers at night, and is a complainer. There's only one way to shut up a screech owl; you lay a broom across the open kitchen door. Granma done this and I've never seen it fail. The screech owl will always stop complaining.

The joe ree only sings in the day, and he is called jo-ree because that is all he ever sings . . . jo-ree . . . over and over, but if he comes close to the cabin, he is a certain sign that you will not get sick atall for the entire summer.

The blue jay playing around the cabin means you are going to have plenty of good times and fun. The blue jay is a clown and bounces on the ends of branches and turns flips and teases other birds.

The red cardinal means you are going to get some money, and the turtledove don't mean to mountain folk what they mean to a sharecropper. When you hear a turtledove, it means that somebody loves you and has sent the turtledove to tell you.

The mourning dove calls late at night and never comes close. He calls from far back in the mountain and it is a long, lonesome call that sounds like he is mourning. Granpa said he is. He said if a feller died and didn't have anybody in the whole world to remember him and cry for him, the mourning dove would remember and mourn. Granpa said if you died somewheres far off, even across the great waters, that if you was a mountain man you would know you would be remembered by the mourning dove. He said it lent a matter of peace to a feller's mind, knowing that. Which I know it did for my mind.

Granpa said if you recollected somebody you loved who had passed on, then the mourning dove would not have to mourn him. You would know then that he was mourning for somebody else, and they didn't sound might near as lonesome. When I heard him, late at night, while I lay in my bedstead, I would remember Ma. Then I wasn't as lonesome.

Birds, just like everything else, know if you like them. If you do, then they will come all around you. Our mountains and hollows was filled with birds: mockingbirds and flickers, red-winged blackbirds and indian hens, meadowlarks and chip-wills, robins and bluebirds, hummingbirds and martins—so many that there is no way to tell of them all.

We stopped trapping in the spring and summer. Granpa said that there was no way in the world that a feller could mate and fight at the same time. He said animals couldn't either. Granpa said even if they could mate and you hunting them, they could not raise their young, and so you would eventual starve to death. We taken pretty heavy to fishing in the spring and summer.

The Indian never fishes or hunts for sport, only for food. Granpa said it was the silliest damn thing in the world to go around killing something for sport. He said the whole thing, more than likely, was thought up by politicians between wars when they wasn't gittin' people killed so they could keep their hand in on killing. Granpa said that idjits taken it up without a lick of thinking at it, but if you could check it out—politicians started it. Which is likely.

We made fish baskets out of willows. We wove the willows together and made baskets maybe three feet long. At the mouth of the basket, we turned the willow ends down and sharpened them into points. This way, the fish could swim into the basket, and the little ones could swim back out, but the big fish couldn't come out through the sharp points. Granma baited the baskets with meal balls.

Sometimes we baited them with fiddle worms. You get fiddle worms by driving a stob in the ground and rubbing, or "fiddling," a board across the top of the stob. The fiddler worms will come out on top of the ground.

We toted the baskets up the Narrows to the creek.

There we tied them with a line to a tree and lowered them into the water. The next day we would come back and get our fish.

There would be big catfish and bass in the basket . . . sometimes a brim, and once I got a trout in my basket. Sometimes we caught turtles in the baskets. They are good when cooked with mustard greens. I liked to pull up the baskets.

Granpa taught me to hand fish. This was how, the second time in my five years of living, I nearly got killed. The first time, of course, was working in the whiskey trade when the tax law might near caught me. I was more than certain sure they would have taken me to the settlement and hanged me. Granpa said, more than likely they wouldn't have as he had never knowed such case to happen. But Granpa didn't see them. They wasn't chasing him. This time, however, Granpa nearly got killed too.

It was in the middle of the day, which is the best time to hand fish. The sun hits the middle of the creek and the fish move back under the banks to lie in the cool and doze.

This is when you lay down on the creek bank and ease your hands into the water and feel for the fish holes. When you find one, you bring your hands in easy and slow, until you feel the fish. If you are patient, you can rub your hands along the sides of the fish and he will lie in the water while you rub him.

Then you take one hold behind his head, the other on his tail, and lift him out of the water. It takes some time to learn.

This day, Granpa was laying on the bank and had already pulled a catfish out of the water. I couldn't find a fish hole, so I went a ways down the bank. I lay down and eased my hands into the water, feeling for a fish hole. I heard a sound right by me. It was a dry rustle that started slow and got faster until it made a whirring noise.

I turned my head toward the sound. It was a rattlesnake.

He was coiled to strike, his head in the air, and looking down on me, not six inches from my face. I froze stiff and couldn't move. He was bigger around than my leg and I could see ripples moving under his dry skin. He was mad. Me and the snake stared at each other. He was flicking out his tongue—nearly in my face—and his eyes was slitted—red and mean.

The end of his tail began to flutter faster and faster; making the whirring sound get higher. Then his head, shaped like a big V, begun to weave just a little, back and forth, for he was deciding what part of my face to hit. I knew he was about to strike me but I couldn't move.

A shadow fell on the ground over me and the snake. I hadn't heard him coming atall but I knew it was Granpa. Soft and easy, like he was remarking about the weather, Granpa said, "Don't turn yer head. Don't move, Little Tree. Don't blink yer eyes." Which I didn't. The snake raised his head higher, getting ready to hit me. I thought he would not stop raising up.

Then, of a sudden, Granpa's big hand come between my face and the snake's head. The hand stayed there. The rattler drew up higher. He begun to hiss, and rattled a solid whirring sound. If Granpa had moved his hand . . . or flinched, the snake would have hit me square in the face. I knew it too.

But he didn't. The hand stayed steady as a rock. I could see the big veins on the back of Granpa's hand. There was beads of sweat standing out too, shining against the copper skin. There wasn't a tremble nor a shake in the hand.

The rattler struck, fast and hard. He hit Granpa's hand like a bullet; but the hand never moved atall. I saw the needle fangs bury up in the meat as the rattler's jaws took up half his hand.

Granpa moved his other hand, and grabbed the rattler behind the head, and he squeezed. The rattler come up off the ground and wrapped himself around and around Granpa's arm. He thrashed at Granpa's head with his rattling end, and beat him in the face with it. But Granpa wouldn't turn loose. He choked that snake to death with one hand, until I heard the crack of backbone. Then he throwed him on the ground.

Granpa set down and whipped out his long knife. He reached over and cut big slashes in his hand where the snake had bit. Blood was running over his hand and down his arm. I crawled over to Granpa . . . for I was weak as dishwater, and didn't think I could walk. I pulled myself to standing by holding onto Granpa's shoulder. He was sucking the blood out of the knife slash and spitting it on the ground. I didn't know what to do, so I said, "Thankee, Granpa." Granpa looked at me and grinned. He had blood smeared over his mouth and face.

"Helldamnfire!" Granpa said. "We showed that son of a bitch, didn't we?"

"Yes, sir," I said, feeling better about the whole thing. "We showed that son of a bitch." Though I couldn't rightly recall as having much to do with the showing.

Granpa's hand commenced to get bigger and bigger. It was turning blue. He taken his long knife and split the sleeve of his deer shirt. The arm was twice as big as his other one. I got scared.

Granpa taken off his hat and fanned his face. "Hot as hell," he said, "fer this time of year." His face looked funny. Now his arm was turning blue.

"I'm going for Granma," I said. I started off. Granpa looked after me and his eyes stared off, faraway.

"Reckin I'll rest a spell," he said, calm as syrup. "I'll be along directly."

I run down the Narrows trail, and I guess maybe that nothing but my toes touched the ground. I couldn't see good, for my eyes was blinded with tears though I didn't cry. When I turned onto the hollow trail, my chest was burning like fire. I commenced to fall down, running down the hollow trail, sometimes in the spring branch, but I scrambled right up again. I left the trail and cut through briers and bushes. I knew Granpa was dying .

The cabin looked crazy and tilted when I run into the clearing, and I tried to yell for Granma . . . but nothing would come out. I fell through the kitchen door and right into Granma's arms. Granma held me and put cold water on my face. She looked at me steady and said, "What happened—where?" I tried to get it out. "Granpa's dying . . ." I whispered, "rattlesnake . . . creek bank." Granma dropped me flat on the floor, which knocked the rest of the wind out of me.

She grabbed a sack and was gone. I can see her now; full skirt, with hair braids flying behind and her tiny moccasin feet flying over the ground. She could run! She had not said anything, "Oh Lord!" or nothing. She never hesitated nor looked around. I was on my hands and knees in the kitchen door, and I hollered after her, "Don't let Granpa die!" She never slowed down, running from the clearing up the trail. I screamed as loud as I could, and it echoed up the hollow, "Don't let him die, Granma!" I figured, more than likely, Granma wouldn't let him die.

I turned the dogs out and they took off after Granma, howling and baying up the trail. I ran behind them, fast as I could.

When I got there, Granpa was laying flat out. Granma had propped his head up, and the dogs was circling around, whining. Granpa's eyes was closed and his arm was nearly black.

Granma had slashed his hand again and was sucking on it, spitting blood on the ground. When I stumbled up, she pointed to a birch tree. "Pull the bark off, Little Tree."

I grabbed Granpa's long knife and stripped the bark off the tree. Granma built a fire, using the birch bark to start it, for it will burn like paper. She dipped water out

of the creek and hung a can over the fire and commenced
to put roots and seeds into it; and some leaves that she
had taken from the sack. I don't know all of what was used,
but the leaves was lobelia, for Granma said that Granpa
had to have it to help him breathe.

Granpa's chest was moving slow and hard. While the
can was heating, Granma stood and looked around. I hadn't
seen anything atall . . . but fifty yards off, against the
mountain, there was a quail nesting on the ground. Granma
undid her big skirt and let it drop on the ground. She
hadn't anything on under it. Her legs looked like a girl's,
with long muscles moving under the copper skin.

She tied the top of the skirt together, and tied rocks
around in the bottom of the skirt. Then she moved on the
quail's nest like a wind whisper. Just at the right time—
she knew—the quail rose off the nest, and she threw the
skirt over it.

She brought the quail back, and while it was still alive,
she split it from breastbone to tail, and spraddled it,
kicking, over Granpa's snake bite. She held the kicking
quail on Granpa's hand for a long time, and when she took
it off, the quail had turned green all over its inside. It was
poison from the snake.

The evening wore on, and Granma worked over Granpa.
The dogs set around us in a circle, watching. Nighttime
fell, and Granma had me build up the fire. She said we
had to keep Granpa warm and couldn't move him. She
taken her skirt and laid it over him. I taken off my
deer shirt and laid it on him too, and was taking off
my britches, but Granma said that wasn't necessary, as
my britches wasn't hardly big enough to cover one of
Granpa's feet. Which they wasn't.

I kept the fire going. Granma had me build another
fire near Granpa's head and so I kept them both going.
Granma laid down by Granpa, holding close to him, for she
said her body heat would help . . . and so I laid by Granpa

on the other side; though I reckined my body wasn't hardly big enough to heat up much of Granpa. But Granma said I helped. I told Granma I didn't see hardly any way atall that Granpa would die.

I told her how it all happened, and that I reckined it was my fault for not watching. Granma said it wasn't anybody's fault, not even the rattlesnake's. She said we wasn't to place fault ner gain on anything that just happened. Which made me feel some better, but not much.

Granpa commenced to talk. He was a boy again, running through the mountains, and he told all about it. Granma said this was because he was recollecting while he was sleeping. He talked, off and on, all night. Just before dawn, he quietened and begun to breathe easy and regular. I told Granma the way I see it, there wasn't might near any way atall that Granpa could die now. She said he wasn't going to. So I went to sleep in the crook of his arm.

I woke at sunup . . . just as the first light topped the mountain. Granpa set up, all of a sudden. He looked down at me, and then at Granma. He said, "By God! Bonnie Bee, a feller can't lay his body down nowheres without you stripping buck naked and hunching at 'em."

Granma slapped Granpa's face and laughed. She rose and put on her skirt. I knew Granpa was all right. He wouldn't leave for home until he had skinned the rattler. He said Granma would make a belt for me, from its skin. Which she did.

We headed down the Narrows trail for the cabin, the dogs running ahead. Granpa was a little weak-kneed, and held Granma close, helping him to walk, I reckined. I trotted along behind them, feeling might near the best I had ever felt since coming to the mountains.

Though Granpa never mentioned putting his hand between me and the snake, I figured, next to Granma, more than likely Granpa kinned me more than anybody else in the world, even Blue Boy.

The Farm in the Clearing

THAT NIGHT by the creek, laying next to Granpa, I guess I was surprised to find out Granpa had ever been a boy. But he had.

Through the night, his mind taken him back, and he was a boy again. Granpa was nine years old in 1867. He had the run of the mountains. His Ma was Red Wing, full Cherokee, and he was raised like all Cherokee young, which meant he could ramble as he pleased in the mountains.

The land was occupied by Union soldiers and run by politicians. Granpa's Pa had fought on the losing side. He had enemies . . . and so didn't venture out of the mountains hardly any atall. Granpa run errands to the settlement when it was needed, for nobody paid any attention to an Indian boy.

It was on one of his ramblings that Granpa found the little valley. It was deep between high mountains and growed up with weeds and bushes and tangled over with vines. Nothing had been planted in the valley in a long time, but Granpa could tell that once it had been planted, for it was cleared of trees.

An old house set at the end of the valley, close to the mountains. It had a sagging porch and bricks falling off the chimney and for a while Granpa paid no attention to the house. Then he commenced to see life around it and knew somebody was living in it. He slipped down closer, off the mountain, to watch through the bushes at the people around the house. They wasn't much.

There wasn't a chicken on the place, like most white people had, or a cow for milking, nor a mule for plowing. There wasn't anything except some broke-down farming tools laying aside an old barn. The people looked about like the place.

The woman looked frailed and wore-out to Granpa. She had two young'uns who looked worse; little girls with old faces. They was dirty and had stringy hair and legs like canes.

An old black man lived in the barn. He was bald with a white fringe of hair around his head. Granpa figured he was dying, for he shuffled along, barely walking, and he was stooped over toward the ground.

Granpa had been about to turn away when he saw somebody else. It was a man wearing what was left of a ragged gray uniform. He was tall and he had one leg. He come out of the house, stabbing along on a hickory sapling that he had strapped to the stump of his other leg. Granpa watched while the one-legged man and the woman walked to the barn. They strapped leather harness on themselves, and Granpa couldn't figure what they was doing until he saw them going to the valley in front of the house.

The old black man followed them. He was staggering along, trying to hold up plow stocks. They got in front of the house and commenced to bend and pull in their harness. The old black man tried to guide the plow. Granpa thought they was crazy, trying to pull a plow like a mule. But they pulled it. Not very far at a time—only a few steps—but they pulled it. They would stop and start again.

They wasn't doing much good. If the old black man

tilted the plow too much, it went deep in the ground, so they couldn't pull, and so they would have to back up, while the old black pulled and hauled at the plow, falling down and getting up again, trying to get the plow set again. It was too shallow for real turning of land. Granpa figured they would never get it plowed.

He left that evening, while they was still at it, pulling and tugging. He come back the next morning to watch. They was in the field when Granpa got to his hiding place. They hadn't plowed enough ground to even see over the weeds. While Granpa watched, the plow point hung under a root and jerked the old black man down. He stayed down a long time on his hands and knees before he got back up. That's when Granpa saw the Union soldiers.

He moved back into a deep fern growth and kept his eye on them. They didn't scare him, for though he was only nine years old, Granpa was Indian-wise, and could move right through the whole patrol without them seeing him, and he knew it.

There was a dozen men in the patrol, all on horseback. A big man with stripes of yellow on his arms was leading them, and they were stopped back in a pine grove, watching the plowing too. They watched for a while, then rode on out of sight.

Granpa went hand fishing on a creek, and come back by late that evening with his fish. They was still at it, but going so slow and tired they was practical crawling. Then Granpa's hawk eyes caught the yellow flash in the trees. It was the Union patrol leader, back in the pines. He was by himself and he was watching again. Granpa slipped onto a back trail to home.

That night he got to figuring. He figured the Union soldier with the yellow stripes was up to meanness, and he determined he would warn the people in the old house that they was being watched. Next morning, he set himself to do just that.

He got to his hiding place, but Granpa was shy of people. He waited, trying to figure how to go about it. They was out in the field, jerking at the old plow again. He had about decided he would leap out in the field, holler what he wanted to tell them, and then run. But he was too late; he saw the Union soldier with the yellow stripes.

He was still a ways off in the pines, and he had another horse with him but nobody was on it. As he come closer, Granpa saw it was not a horse but a mule. It was the worst looking mule Granpa had ever seen; hip bones sticking out, and ribs. Its ears flopped down over its bony face, but it was a mule. The Union soldier was driving the old mule ahead of him. Just as he got to the edge of the woods, the soldier strapped the old mule with a whip, and it taken out across the field. The soldier stayed back in the woods on his horse.

The woman saw the mule first. She dropped her harness and stared at the mule running across the field. Then she hollered, "Lord God almighty! H'it's a mule. He's sent us a mule!" She taken out after the mule, running through the bushes. The old black man taken out too, running and falling, trying to catch up.

The mule run straight toward where Granpa was hiding. When it got close, Granpa jumped up and waved his arms and the mule swerved back into the field and headed for the woods over to one side. The soldier had circled his horse in the woods, and he scared the mule back into the field. Neither Granpa nor the soldier was noticed, for the woman and the old black man had their eyes on the mule.

The one-legged man was trying to run, stumping his hickory sapling into the ground, and falling flat down every few steps. The two young'uns was running, hollering through briers, trying to head the mule off.

The old mule got confused and run back through the whole crowd of them. The woman grabbed his tail. He jerked her off her feet but she held on, the mule dragging her through the bushes, tearing off her dress. The old black man sprung at the mule and got hold on his neck. He was flung around like a rag doll, but he held on like he would die if he turned loose. The old mule give it up and stopped.

The one-legged man and the young'uns come up. He put a leather strap around the old mule's head. They all walked around the old mule, petting him and rubbing him like he was the finest mule in the the world. Granpa thought the old mule commenced to feel pretty good about the whole thing.

Then they all knelt down in the field in a circle around the old mule, and stayed a good while that way, with their heads turned to the ground.

Granpa watched them hitch the mule to the plow. First one would plow behind the mule then another'n—even the young'uns. Granpa watched from the bushes and kept his eye on the soldier watching them from the woods.

The valley got to be something that Granpa kept watch on right regular. He had to see how the plowing would come out. In three days' time, they had turned a quarter of the field.

On the morning of the fourth day, Granpa saw the Union soldier drop a white sack at the end of the field. The one-legged man saw him too. He half lifted his hand to wave, like he wasn't sure he'd ought to. The Union soldier done the same, and rode off into the woods. It was a sack of seed corn.

The next morning, when Granpa got to the valley, the Union soldier was dismounted in front of the house. He was talking with the one-legged man and the old black man. Granpa edged in close to hear them.

In a little while the Union soldier was plowing the old mule. He had the plow lines tied and looped around his neck, and Granpa could tell he knew his business. Every once in a while, he would stop the mule. He would reach down and get a handful of fresh turned earth and smell of it. Sometimes he would even taste it. Then he would crumble the dirt in his hand and start plowing again.

Turned out, he was a sergeant, and he was a farmer from Illinois. Usually, he couldn't show up to plow until nearly sundown, when he could slip away from the army post. But he come and plowed nearly every day.

One evening he brought a skinny private with him. He looked too young to be in the army, but he was. He commenced coming with the sergeant every evening. He brought little bushes with him. They was apple trees.

He would set one out on the edge of the field and work at it for an hour, getting it set in and watered. He would pat the ground around it, prune it up, fix frames of wood to put around it, and then set back and look at it like it was the first apple tree he had ever seen.

The two little girls taken to helping him, and in a month's time he had completely ringed the field with apple trees. Turned out, he was from New York and come from apple raising as his trade. By the time he had all his apple trees put out, the rest of them had the entire valley planted in corn.

Granpa left a dozen catfish on the front porch after dark one time. The next evening, they cooked the catfish and was eating them off a table set under a tree in the yard. Occasionally, while they was eating, the sergeant or the woman would stand up and wave toward the mountains, inviting Granpa in. They knew an Indian had left the fish but they could never spot Granpa, they just waved at the mountains. Not being Indian, they could never tell how to separate a wrong color from the woods around it. Granpa never went in. He left them some more fish, though. He would hang the fish on tree limbs near the yard, for he was afraid to go on the front porch anymore.

Granpa said he left them the fish because, them not being Indian, and so being ignorant, they would likely total starve to death before they could get their crop in.

And too, he was not, nowise, going to be outdone by a Union soldier, ner any two of them, though he drawed the line at crop raising, not taken up too favorable with plowing and such.

The skinny private and the little girls drawed water from the well at dusk every evening. They toted buckets, sloshing water, and watered every apple tree. This went on while the other was hoeing and thinning the corn. Granpa realized the Union sergeant was as total crazy about hoeing as he had been about plowing. The corn was up, dark green, which meant it was a good corn crop. The apple trees taken to sprigging green.

It was summer then; the days long, and dusk evening slow in coming. The sergeant and the private could get in two or three hours work before they had to leave and go back to the army post.

In the cool of the dusk, just as the whippoorwills started to sing, they would all stand in the front yard and look out over the field. The sergeant smoked his pipe, and the two little girls stood close as they could to the skinny private. His hands was always caked with dirt from clawing around his apple trees, for he would not trust a hoe to work around them.

The sergeant would take his pipe in his hand. "It's good land," he would say with his eyes on the field like he would eat the ground if he could.

"Yes," the one-legged man would say, "it's good land."

"Best corn crop I ever seed," the old black man would say. He would say it every evening. Granpa said he slipped close, but all they ever done was stand and stare at the fields . . . and say the same things every evening, like the field was some kind of natural wonder they was all supposed to stare at. The skinny private would always say, "Wait a year—when them apple trees start blooming . . . you ain't never seen nothing like it." The little girls would giggle, which made them look younger.

The sergeant would point with his pipe. "Now next year, you'll want to clear that little neck of brush against the far mountain. It'll make maybe three, four acres of corn."

Granpa could see the little valley was looking might near like there was nothing else could be done to it. He said it looked like they had everything set. He commenced to lose interest in the whole thing. But then the Regulators come.

They rode in one evening when the sun was still high, a dozen of them. They had fancy uniforms and guns, and represented the politicians who passed new-set laws and raised taxes.

Riding up to the house yard, they planted a pole in the yard, and on top of the pole they put a red flag. Granpa knew what the red flag meant. He had seen it around in the settlements. It meant some politician wanted your property, and so they raised the taxes on it high enough that you couldn't pay it. Then they put up the red flag, meaning they was going to take it over.

The one-legged man, the woman, and the old black man and the young'uns, all come out of the field with their hoes when they saw the Regulators. They bunched up in the yard. Granpa saw the one-legged man throw down his hoe and go in the house. In a minute, he stumped back out and he had an old musket in his hands. He pointed it at the Regulators.

The Union sergeant rode up. The skinny private wasn't with him. The sergeant got off his horse and stepped between the Regulators and the one-legged man. About that time, a Regulator fired his gun, and the sergeant staggered back, looking surprised and hurt. His hat tumbled off his head, and he fell to the ground.

The one-legged man shot off his musket and hit a Regulator, and the Regulators commenced firing their guns. They killed the one-legged man and he fell off the porch. The woman and little girls run screaming to him. They tried to prop him up but Granpa knew he was dead, for his neck was limp.

Granpa saw the old black man run at the Regulators with his hoe raised up in the air. They shot him two or three times and he fell, laying over his hoe handle. Then they rode off.

Granpa took to the back trail, for he was sure they would circle about, making to know that they hadn't been seen. He told his Pa about it and expected there would be trouble over it, but there wasn't.

Granpa found out in the settlement how it was passed off. The politicians passed it out that it looked like an uprising, and they was going to have to be reelected to handle it and get more money for what looked like a war. People got worked up about it, and told the politicians to go to it. Which they did.

A rich man took over the valley. Granpa never knew what happened to the woman and the young'uns. The rich man brought in sharecroppers. The land and weather being as it is, you can't raise apples in big enough bunches to make real money, so they plowed up the apple trees.

Word was passed that a private from New York deserted the army. He was posted as a coward, running out on a uprising and all.

Granpa said they boxed the sergeant up to send his remains and such back to Illinois. He said when they went to fix him and dress him, one of his hands was clenched into a fist. They tried to unclench the fist, and finally had to take tools to do it. They got his fist open, but there wasn't anything in it worthwhile. Nothing but a handful of black dirt fell out.

A Night on the Mountain

ME AND GRANPA thought Indian. Later people would tell me that this is naive—but I knew—and I remembered what Granpa said about "words." If it is "naive," it does not matter, for it is also good. Granpa said it would always carry me through . . . which it has; like the time the big-city men made a trip to our mountains.

Granpa was half Scot, but he thought Indian. Such seemed to be the case with others, like the great Red Eagle, Bill Weatherford, or Emperor McGilvery or McIntosh. They gave themselves, as the Indian did, to nature, not trying to subdue it, or pervert it, but to live with it. And so they loved the thought, and loving it grew to be it, so that they could not think as the white man.

Granpa told me. The Indian brought something to trade and laid it at the white man's feet. If he saw nothing he wanted, he picked up his wares and walked off. The white man, not understanding, called him an "Indian giver" meaning one who gives and then takes back. This is not so. If the Indian gives a gift, he will make no ceremony of it, but will simply leave it to be found.

Granpa said the Indian held his palm up to show

"peace," that he held no weapon. This was logical to
Granpa but seemed funny as hell to everybody else.
Granpa said the white man meant the same thing by
shaking hands, except his words was so crooked, he had to
try to shake a weapon out of the sleeve of the feller who
claimed he was a friend. Granpa was not given much to
handshaking, as he said he didn't like for a man to try
to shake something out of his sleeve after he had presented
himself as a friend. It was total distrustful of a man's word.
Which is reasonable.

As to folks saying, "How!" and then laughing when they
see an Indian, Granpa said it all come about over a couple
of hundred years. He said every time the Indian met a
white man, the white man commenced to ask him: *how*
are you feeling, or *how* are your people, or *how* are you
getting along, or *how* is the game where you come from,
and so on. He said the Indian come to believe that the
white man's favorite subject was *how*; and so, being polite,
when he met the white man, he figured he would just
say *how*, and then let the son of a bitch talk about whichever *how* he wanted to. Granpa said people laughing at
that was laughing at an Indian who was trying to be
courteous and considerate.

We had delivered our wares to the crossroads store and
Mr. Jenkins said two big-city men had been there. He
said they was from Chattanooga and drove a long black
automobile. Mr. Jenkins said they wanted to talk to
Granpa.

Granpa looked at Mr. Jenkins from under his big hat.
"Tax-law?"

"No," Mr. Jenkins said. "They wasn't law atall. Said
they was in the whiskey trade. Said they heard tell you
was a good maker and they wanted to put you in a big
still, and that you could get rich working for them."

Granpa didn't say anything. He bought some coffee and
sugar for Granma. I picked up the wood chips and taken

the old candy off Mr. Jenkins' hands. Mr. Jenkins fidgeted around to hear what Granpa had to say about it, but he knew Granpa too well to ask.

"They said they would be back." Mr. Jenkins said.

Granpa bought some cheese . . . which I was glad, as I liked cheese. We walked out, and didn't hang around the store; but headed straight off up the trail. Granpa walked fast. I hadn't time to pick berries and had to do away with the old candy while I was in a continual trot behind Granpa.

When we got to the cabin Granpa told Granma about the big-city men. He said, "You stay here, Little Tree. I'm going to the still and lay some more covering branches over it. If they come, you let me know." He taken off, up the hollow trail.

I set on the front porch watching for the big-city men. Granpa had not hardly gone from sight when I saw them and told Granma. Granma stayed back, standing in the dogtrot, and we watched them coming up the trail and across the foot log.

They had fine clothes like politicians. The big fat man wore a lavender suit and white tie. The skinny man had on a white suit and black shirt which shined. They wore big-city hats made of fine straw.

They walked right up to the porch, though they didn't mount the steps. The big man was sweating pretty bad. He looked at Granma. "We want to see the old man," he said. I figured he was sick, for his breathing was bad and it was hard to see his eyes. His eyes looked slitted, way back in swelled-up fat.

Granma didn't say anything. I didn't either. The big man turned around to the skinny man. "The old squaw don't understand English, Slick."

Mr. Slick was looking around over his shoulder, though I didn't see anything behind him. He had a high voice. "Screw the old squaw," he said, "I don't like this place,

Chunk—too far back in the mountains. Let's get outa here." Mr. Slick had a little mustache.

"Shut up," Mr. Chunk said. Mr. Chunk pushed his hat back. He didn't have any hair. He looked at me setting in the chair.

"The boy looks like a breed," he said. "Maybe he understands English. Do you understand English, boy?"

I said, "I reckin."

Mr. Chunk looked at Mr. Slick. "Hear that . . . he reckins." They got tickled about this and laughed right loud about it. I saw Granma move back and turn Blue Boy out. He headed up the hollow for Granpa.

Mr. Chunk said, "Where's your Pa, boy?" I told him I didn't recollect my Pa; that I lived here with Granpa and Granma. Mr. Chunk wanted to know where Granpa was, and I pointed back up the trail. He reached in his pocket and took out a whole dollar and held it out toward me. "You can have this dollar, boy, if you take us to your Granpa."

He had big rings on his fingers. I seen right off that he was rich and more than likely could afford the dollar. I taken it and put it in my pocket. I knew figures pretty well. Even splitting with Granpa, I would get back the fifty cents which I had been slickered out of by the Christian.

I felt pretty good about the whole thing, leading them up the trail. But as we walked. I commenced to think. I couldn't take them to the still. I led them up the high trail.

As we walked up the high trail, I felt kind of bad about it, and I didn't have any idea in the world what I was going to do. Mr. Chunk and Mr. Slick, however, was in fine spirits. They pulled off their coats and walked long behind me. Each one had a pistol in his belt. Mr. Slick said, "Don't remember your Pa, huh kid?" I stopped and said I hadn't no recollection of him atall. Mr. Slick said, "That would make you a bastard, wouldn't it, kid?" I said

I reckined, though I had not got to the B's in the dictionary and had not studied that word. They both laughed until
they commenced coughing. I laughed too. They seemed
like happy fellers.

Mr. Chunk said, "Hell, they're all a bunch of animals."
I said we had lots of animals in the mountains . . . wildcats and wild hogs; and me and Granpa had seen a black
bear oncet.

Mr. Slick wanted to know if we had seen one lately. I
said we hadn't but we had seen signs. I pointed to a
poplar tree where a bear had taken a claw swipe. "There's
sign right there," I said. Mr. Chunk jumped sideways like
a snake had struck at him. He bumped into Mr. Slick and
knocked him down. Mr. Slick got mad. "Goddam you,
Chunk, you nearly knocked me off the trail! If you had
knocked me down there . . ." Mr. Slick pointed down into
the hollow. Him and Mr. Chunk both leaned over and
looked down. You could barely see the spring branch, far
below us.

"God almighty," Mr. Chunk said, "how high are we?
Hell, if you slipped off this trail, you'd break your neck."
I told Mr. Chunk I didn't know how high we was, but I
reckined it was pretty high; though I had never give any
thought to it.

The higher we got, the more Mr. Chunk and Mr. Slick
coughed. They also fell farther and farther behind me. Once
I come back down the trail looking for them, and they
were sprawled out under a white oak. The white oak had
poison ivy all around its roots. They was laying in the
middle of it.

Poison ivy is pretty and green, but you had better not
lay in it. It will pop welts out all over you and make sores
that will last for months. I didn't say anything about the
poison ivy. They was already in it anyway, and I didn't
want to make them feel worse about things. They was
looking pretty bad.

Mr. Slick raised his head up. "Listen, you little bastard,"

he said, "how much farther we got to go?" Mr. Chunk didn't raise his head. He laid there in the poison ivy with his eyes closed. I said we was nearly there.

I had been thinking. I knew that Granma would send Granpa up the high trail after me, so when we got to the top of the mountain, I was going to tell Mr. Slick and Mr. Chunk that we would just set down and wait; that Granpa would be along directly. Which he would. I figured it would work all right and I could keep the dollar, seeing as how I would have, more or less, taken them to Granpa.

I set off up the trail. Mr. Slick helped Mr. Chunk out of the poison ivy patch and they kind of staggered along behind me. They left their coats in the patch. Mr. Chunk said they would get the coats on the way back.

I got to the top of the mountain a long time before they did. The high trail was part of a lot of trails, old Cherokee trails that ran along the rim of the mountain, but forked, going down the mountain on the other side, and forked four or five times on the way down. Granpa said the trails led maybe a hundred miles back into the mountains.

I set down under a bush where the trail made a fork; one branch running the top of the mountain, the other dipping over the mountain down the other side. I figured I would wait on Mr. Chunk and Mr. Slick, and we would all set here until Granpa come.

It took them a long time. When they finally come over the top of the mountain, Mr. Chunk had his arm over Mr. Slick's shoulders. He had hurt his foot, more than likely, for he was limping and hopping pretty bad.

Mr. Chunk was saying that Mr. Slick was a bastard. Which surprised me, as Mr. Slick had not said anything about being a bastard too. Mr. Chunk was saying that Mr. Slick was the one who originally thought up the idea of putting mountain hicks to work for them. Mr. Slick said it was Mr. Chunk's idea to pick this dam Indian and that Mr. Chunk was a son of a bitch.

They was talking so loud, they passed right by me. I didn't have a chance to tell them we had all ought to wait, as Granpa had learnt me not to interrupt when people was talking. They went on down the trail on the other side of the mountain. I watched them until they disappeared amongst the trees, heading into a deep cleft between the mountains. I figured I had better wait on Granpa.

I didn't have to wait long. Blue Boy showed up first. I saw him sniffing my trail, and he come up, tail wagging. In a minute I heard a whippoorwill. It sounded exactly like a whippoorwill . . . but as it was not dusk dark yet, I knew it was Granpa. I whippoorwilled back, might near as good.

I saw his shadow slipping through the trees in the late evening sun. He wasn't following the trail, and you could never hear him, if he didn't want to be heard. In a minute there he was. I was glad to see him.

I told Granpa that Mr. Slick and Mr. Chunk had gone on down the trail, and also everything I could remember they said while we was walking. Granpa grunted and didn't say anything, but his eyes narrowed down.

Granma had sent us vittles in a sack, and me and Granpa set down under a cedar and ate. Corn pone and catfish cooked in meal taste good in the air of a high mountain. We finished off all of it.

I showed Granpa the dollar, which I reckined if Mr. Chunk figured I had done my job I could keep. I told Granpa soon as we got some change we could split it. Granpa said I had done my job, as he was here to see Mr. Chunk. Granpa said I could keep the whole dollar.

I told Granpa about the green and red box at Mr. Jenkins' store. I said I figured, more than likely, it wasn't much over a dollar. Granpa said he figured that too. Far off, we heard a yell down in the cleft of the mountain. We had plumb forgot about Mr. Chunk and Mr. Slick.

It was getting dusk dark. Whippoorwills and chip-wills had started singing on the side of the mountain. Granpa stood up and cupped his hands around his mouth. "WHOOOOOOOOEEEEEEEEEE!" Granpa hollered down the mountain. The sound bounced off another mountain as plain as if Granpa had been over there; then it bounced into the cleft and on up the hollows, getting weaker and weaker. There wasn't any way of figuring where the sound had come from. The echoes had barely died away when we heard three gun shots from down in the cleft. The sound bounced around and traveled off.

"Pistols," Granpa said. "They're answering with pistol fire."

Granpa cut loose again. "WHOOOOOOEEEEEEEEE!" I did too. Which both of us hollering made the echoes jump and bounce even more. The pistol went off again, three times.

Me and Granpa kept hollering. It was fun, listening to the echoes. Each time the pistol answered us, until it didn't answer the last time.

"They're out of bullets," Granpa said. It was dark now. Granpa stretched and yawned. "No need me and ye thrashing around down there tonight, Little Tree, trying to git 'em out. They'll be all right. We'll git 'em tomorrow." Which suited me.

Me and Granpa pulled spring boughs under the cedar tree to sleep on. If you're going to sleep out in the mountains during spring and summer, you had better sleep on spring boughs. If you don't, red bugs will eat you up. Red bugs are so little, you can't hardly see them with the naked eye. They are all over leaves and bushes, by the millions. They will crawl on you and bury up in your skin, causing rashes of bumps to break out all over you. Some years they are worse than others. This was a bad red bug year. There are also wood ticks.

Me and Granpa and Blue Boy crawled up on the spring

boughs. Blue Boy curled up by me and felt warm in the sharp air. The boughs were soft and springy. I commenced yawning.

Me and Granpa clasped our hands behind our heads and watched the moon come up. It was full and yellow, slipping over a far mountain. We could see might near a hundred miles, Granpa said, mountains humping and dipping in the moon spray, making shadows and deep purples in their hollows. Fog drifted along in threads, far below us . . . moving through the hollows, snaking around the sides of the mountains. One little patch of fog would come around the end of a mountain like a silver boat and bump into another one and they would melt together and take off up a hollow. Granpa said the fog looked alive. Which it did.

A mockingbird set up song right near us in a high elm. Far back in the mountains, we heard two wildcats mating. They sounded like they were screaming mad, but Granpa said mating feels so good that cats can't help but scream about it.

I told Granpa I would might near like to sleep on a mountaintop every night. He said he would too. A screech owl screeched down below us, and then there was yells and screams. Granpa said it was Mr. Chunk and Mr. Slick. He said if they didn't settle down, they would disturb practical all the birds and animals on the mountainside. I went to sleep looking at the moon.

Me and Granpa woke at dawn. There is not anything like dawn from the top of the high mountain. Me and Granpa, and Blue Boy too, watched it. The sky was a light gray, and the birds getting up for the new day made fuss and twitters in the trees.

Away across a hundred miles, the mountaintops humped like islands in the fog that floated below us. Granpa pointed to the east and said, "Watch."

Above the rim of the farthest mountain, on the end of

the world, a pink streak whipped across, a paintbrush swept a million miles across the sky. Morning wind picked up and hit our faces and me and Granpa knew the colors and the morning birth had come alive. The paintbrush run up in streaks—red, yellow and blue. The mountain rim looked like it had caught fire; then the sun cleared the trees. It turned the fog into a pink ocean, heaving and moving down below.

The sun hit me and Granpa in the face. The world had got born all over again. Granpa said it had, and he taken off his hat and we watched it for a long time. Me and Granpa had a feeling, and I knew right off that we would come again to the mountaintop and watch the morning come.

The sun cleared the mountain and floated free in the sky, and Granpa sighed and stretched. "Well," he said, "ye and me have got work to do. Tell ye what," Granpa scratched his head, "tell ye what," he said again, "ye trot down to the cabin and tell Granma we'll be up here awhile. Tell her to fix ye and me something to eat and put it in a paper sack, and fix them two big-city fellers something to eat and put it in a tow sack. Can ye remember now— paper sack and tow sack?" I said I could. I started off.

Granpa stopped me. "And Little Tree," he said, and commenced grinning about something, "before Granma fixes the two fellers something to eat, ye tell everything ye can recollect that the two fellers said to ye." I said I would, and I set off down the trail. Blue Boy went with me. I heard Granpa commence to call up Mr. Chunk and Mr. Slick. Granpa was yelling, "WHOOOOOOOOOEEEEEEEEE!" I would have liked to stayed and hollered too, but I didn't mind running down the trail, especially early in the morning.

This was the time of morning when all the creatures were coming out for the day living. I saw two 'coons, high in a walnut tree. They peeped down at me and talked as I passed under them. Squirrels chattered and leapt across the trail. They set up and fussed at me as I walked by. Birds dipped and fluttered all along the trail, and a mockingbird followed me and Blue Boy a long way, dipping down at my head, teasing. Mockingbirds will do this if they know you like them. Which I do.

When I got to the cabin clearing, Granma was setting on the back porch. She knew I was coming, I figured, by watching the birds, though I suspicioned that Granma could smell anybody coming, for she was never surprised.

I told her Granpa wanted something to eat in a paper sack for me and him, and for Mr. Chunk and Mr. Slick, something to be put in a tow sack. Granma commenced to cook up the vittles.

She had fixed mine and Granpa's, and was frying fish for Mr. Chunk and Mr. Slick, when I recollected to tell her what they had said. While I was telling her, of a sudden she pulled the frying pan off the fire and got out a pot which she filled with water. She dropped Mr. Chunk and Mr. Slick's fish in the pot. I reckined she had decided to boil their fish instead of frying, but I had never seen her use the root powders, in cooking, that she put in their pot. Their fish got a good boiling.

I told Granma Mr. Chunk and Mr. Slick 'peared to be good spirited fellers. I told her that I originally thought we was all laughing because I was a bastard, but it turned out, what they was more than likely laughing at was Mr. Slick's being one too, as I had heard Mr. Chunk remind him.

Granma put some more root powders in the pot. I told her about the dollar—that Granpa said I had done my job and could keep it. Granma said I could keep it too. She put the dollar in my fruit jar for me but I didn't tell her about the red and green box. There was not any Christians about, as I knew of, but I wasn't going to take any chances.

Granma boiled the fish until the steam got heavy. Her

eyes was watering down over her face and she was blowing her nose. She said she reckined it was the steam. Granma put the fish for the big-city fellers in the tow sack and I set off up the high trail. Granma turned all the hounds out, and they went with me.

When I got to the top of the mountain, I didn't see Granpa. I whistled and he answered from halfway down the other side. I went down the trail. It was narrow and shaded over with trees. Granpa said he had practical called up Mr. Chunk and Mr. Slick out of the cleft. He said they was answering him pretty regular and ought to be coming in sight pretty soon.

Granpa taken their sack of fish and hung it down from a tree limb, right over the trail where they couldn't miss it. Me and Granpa moved back up the trail a ways, and set down under persimmon bushes to eat our dinner. The sun was might near straight up.

Granpa made the dogs lay down, and we eat on our corn pone and fish. Granpa said it had taken him some time to get Mr. Chunk and Mr. Slick to understanding which direction they was to take toward his voice but they was finally coming. Then we saw them.

If I had not known them right well, I couldn't have recollected as having ever seen them before. Their shirts was tore up complete. They had big cuts and scratches over their arms and faces. Granpa said it looked like they had run through brier patches. Granpa said he couldn't figure how they got all the big red lumps on their faces. I didn't say anything—as it was none of my business—but I figured it was from laying in the poison ivy vines. Mr. Chunk had lost a shoe. They come up the trail slow and heads down.

When they saw the tow sack hanging over the trail, they taken it loose from the tree limb and set down. They ate all of Granma's fish, and argued pretty regular over which was getting the most of it. We could hear them plain.

After they finished eating, they stretched out on the trail in the shade. I figured Granpa would go down and get them up, but he didn't. We just set and watched. After a while, Granpa said it was better to let them rest awhile. They didn't rest long.

Mr. Chunk jumped up. He was bent over and holding his stomach. He run into the bushes at the side of the trail and pulled his britches down. He squatted and commenced to yell, "Oh! Goddam! My insides is coming out!" Mr. Slick done the same thing. He yelled too. They groaned and hollered and rolled on the ground. In a little while, both of them crawled out of the bushes and laid down on the trail. They didn't lay down long, but jumped up and done it all over again. They taken on so loud that the dogs got excited and Granpa had to quieten them.

I told Granpa it 'peared to me that they was squatting in a poison ivy patch. Granpa said it looked like they was. Also, I told Granpa, they was wiping theirselves with poison ivy leaves. Granpa said more than likely they was. One time, Mr. Slick run from the trail back into the poison ivy patch but did not get his britches down in time. He commenced to have some trouble after that with flies buzzing over him. This went on for might near an hour. After that, they laid flat out in the trail, resting up. Granpa said more than likely it was something they had ate which didn't agree with them.

Granpa stepped out in the trail and whistled down to them. Both of them got on their hands and knees and looked up toward me and Granpa. Leastwise, I think they looked at us, but their eyes were swelled might near shut. Both of them yelled.

"Wait a minute," Mr. Chunk hollered. Mr. Slick kind of screamed, "Hold on, man—for God's sake!" They got to their feet and scrambled up the trail. Me and Granpa went on up the trail to the top of the mountain. When we looked back, they was limping behind us.

Granpa said we might as well go back down the trail to the cabin, as they could now find their way out, and would be along d'rectly. So we did.

It was late sun by the time me and Granpa got to the cabin. We set on the back porch with Granma and waited for Mr. Chunk and Mr. Slick to come along. It was two hours later and dusk dark when they made it to the clearing. Mr. Chunk had lost his other shoe and 'peared to tiptoe along.

They made a wide circle around the cabin, which surprised me, as I figured they wanted to see Granpa, but they had changed their minds. I asked Granpa about keeping my dollar. He said I could, as I had done my part of the job. It was not my fault if they changed their minds. Which is reasonable.

I followed them around the cabin. They crossed the foot log and I hollered and waved to them, "Good-bye, Mr. Chunk. Good-bye, Mr. Slick. I thankee for the dollar, Mr. Chunk."

Mr. Chunk turned and 'peared to shake his fist at me. He fell off the foot log into the spring branch. He grabbed at Mr. Slick and nearly pulled him off, but Mr. Slick kept his balance and made it across. Mr. Slick reminded Mr. Chunk that he was a son of a bitch, and Mr. Chunk, as he crawled out of the spring branch, said that when he got back to Chattanooga—if he ever did—he was going to kill Mr. Slick. Though I don't know why they had fell out with one another.

They passed out of sight down the hollow trail. Granma wanted to send the dogs after them, but Granpa said no. He said he figured they was total wore out.

Granpa said he reckined it all come about from a misunderstanding on Mr. Chunk and Mr. Slick's part, regarding me and Granpa working for them in the whiskey trade. I figured more than likely it was too.

It had all taken up the best part of two days of mine and

Granpa's time. I had, however, come out a dollar ahead. I cautioned Granpa that I was still willing and stood ready to split the dollar with him as we was partners, but he said no, I had earned the dollar without any connection in the whiskey trade. Granpa said all things considered it was not bad pay for the work. Which it wasn't.

Willow John

PLANTING IS a busy time. Granpa decided when we would begin. He would run his finger into the ground and feel for the warmth; then shake his head, which meant we wasn't going to start planting.

So we would have to go fishing or berry picking or general woods rambling, if it wasn't the week to work at the whiskey trade.

Once you start planting, you have to be careful. There are times when you can't plant. You must begin by remembering that anything growing below ground, such as turnips or 'taters, these have to be planted in the dark by the moon, otherwise your turnips and 'taters won't be any bigger than a pencil.

Anything that grows above ground, such as corn, beans, peas and such, must be planted in the light of the moon. If it isn't, you'll not make much of a crop of it.

When you have figured this out, there are other things. Most people go by the signs in the almanac. For example, you plant running beans when the sign is in the arms to make the best beans. If you don't, you will have a lot of blooms but no beans.

There is a sign for everything. Granpa, however, didn't need an almanac. He went by the stars d'rect.

We would set on the porch in the spring night, and Granpa would study the stars. He would have them set, how they formed on the ridge of the mountain. He would say, "Stars're right for running beans. We'll plant some tomorrow if the east wind ain't blowing." Even with the stars right, Granpa would not plant running beans if the east wind was blowing. He said the beans would not produce.

Then, of course, it could be too wet—or too dry—to plant. If the birds quietened, you didn't plant either. Planting is a pretty tedious proposition.

When we got up in the morning, we might be all set to do some planting, going by the stars the night before. But right off, we would see that the wind was not right or the birds, or it could be too wet or too dry. So we would have to go fishing.

Granma said she suspicioned some of the signs had to do with Granpa's fishing feelings. But Granpa said women couldn't understand complications. He said women thought everything was simple and plain out. Which it wasn't. He said women couldn't help it, because they was born suspicious in the first place. Granpa said he had seen day-old females that looked suspicious at a sucking tit.

When the day was just right, we planted corn mostly. That was our main crop for we depended on it for eating and feeding ol' Sam, and it was our money crop in the whiskey trade.

Granpa laid off the rows with the plow and ol' Sam. I didn't lay off any rows. Granpa said I was mostly a turning plow man. Me and Granma dropped the seeds in the rows and covered them up. On the sides of the mountain Granma planted the corn with a Cherokee planting stick. You just jab it in the ground and drop in the seed.

We planted lots of other things: beans, okra, 'taters, turnips and peas. We planted the peas around the fringe of the patch, near the woods. This attracted deer in the fall. Deer are crazy about peas and will come twenty miles through the mountains to a pea patch. We always got an easy deer for winter meat. We also planted watermelons.

Me and Granpa picked out a shady end of the patch and planted watermelons pretty heavy. Granma said it was a mighty big watermelon patch. But Granpa said what we couldn't eat, we could always tote to the crossroads store and more than likely make a lot of money selling them.

The way it turned out, by the time the watermelons got ripe me and Granpa found out the watermelon market had collapsed. The best you could get for the biggest watermelon you had was a nickel, if you could sell it. Which wasn't likely.

Me and Granpa figgered it out on the kitchen table one evening. Granpa said that a gallon of whiskey weighed about eight or nine pounds, for which we got two dollars; and he didn't hardly see no way in the world that we could tote a twelve-pound watermelon to the crossroads store for a nickel—not unless the whiskey trade fell through, which was not likely. I told Granpa it looked to me like we would have to eat all the watermelons.

Watermelons are might near the slowest growing things ever planted. Beans get ripe—okra—peas—just about everything, and the watermelons just lay there, continually green and growing. I checked on the watermelons fairly heavy.

When you are certain that the watermelons are ripe, they're not. Finding and testing out a ripe watermelon is might near as complicated as planting.

Several times at the supper table I told Granpa that I suspicioned I had found a ripe watermelon. I checked the patch every morning and evening, sometimes at dinnertime too, if I was passing by. Each time, we would go up to the patch and Granpa would check it out. It wouldn't be ready. One evening at the supper table, I told Granpa that I was might near certain that I had found the watermelon we was looking for, and he said we would check it out the next morning.

I was up early, waiting. We got to the patch before sunup and I showed Granpa the watermelon. It was dark green and big. Me and Granpa squatted down by the watermelon and studied it. I had already studied it pretty heavy the evening before, but I went over it again with Granpa. After we studied it awhile, Granpa decided it looked near enough ripe to give it the thump test.

You have to know what you are doing to thump test a watermelon and make any sense out of it. If you thump it and it sounds like a—*think*—it is total green; if it sounds—*thank*—it is green but is coming on; if it goes—*thunk*—then you have got you a ripe watermelon. You have got two chances to one against you, as Granpa said is true in everything.

Granpa thumped the watermelon. He thumped it hard. He didn't say anything, but I was watching his face close and he didn't shake his head, which was a good sign. It didn't mean the watermelon was ripe, but no head shake meant he hadn't give up on it. He thumped it again.

I told Granpa it sounded might near like a *thunk* to me. He set back on his heels and studied it a little more. I did too.

The sun had come up. A butterfly lit on the watermelon and set there, flexing his wings open and closed. I asked Granpa if it wasn't a good sign, since it seems to me I had heard that a butterfly lighting on a watermelon near about made it certain the watermelon was ripe. Granpa said he had never heard of that sign, but it could be true.

He said as near as he could tell, it was a borderline case. He said the sound was somewheres between a *thank* and a *thunk*. I said it sounded like that to me too, but it 'peared to lean pretty heavy toward the *thunk*. Granpa said there was another way we could check it out. He went and got a broom sedge straw.

If you lay a broom sedge straw crosswise on a watermelon and it just lays there, the watermelon is green. But if the broom sedge straw turns from crosswise to lengthwise, then you have got a ripe watermelon. Granpa laid the broom sedge straw on the watermelon. The straw laid there a minute, then it turned a ways and stopped. We set watching it. It wouldn't turn anymore. I told Granpa I believed the straw was too long, which made the ripe inside the watermelon have too much work turning it. Granpa taken the straw off and shortened it. We tried it again. This time it turned more and might near made it lengthwise.

Granpa was ready to give up on it, but I wasn't. I got down so I could watch the straw pretty close, and I told Granpa it 'peared to be moving, slow but steady, toward being lengthwise. Granpa said that could be because I was breathing on it, which didn't count, but he decided not to give up on it. He said if we let it lay until the sun was straight overhead, about dinnertime, then we could pick it from the vine.

I kept a close check on the sun. Seemed like it rolled around and just set on the mountain rim, determined to make a long morning of it. Granpa said the sun acted that way sometimes, like when we was plowing and figuring to go washing in the creek, late of evening.

Granpa said if we got busy doing something, and made out that we didn't give a lick dam about how slow the sun moved, that he would give up and git on with his business. Which we did.

We busied ourselves cutting okra. Okra grows fast and you have to keep it cut. The more okra you cut off a stalk, the more you will have grow back.

I moved along the row ahead of Granpa and cut all the okra that growed low on the stalk. Granpa followed me and cut the high okra. Granpa said he suspicioned that me and him was the only ones who had ever figured how to cut okra without bending over or pulling down the stalks. All morning we cut okra.

We reached the end of a row and there was Granma. She grinned. "Dinnertime," she said. Me and Granpa broke into a run for the watermelon patch. I got there first, and so got to pull the watermelon from the vine. But I couldn't lift it. Granpa carried it to the spring branch and let me roll it in—splosh; it was so heavy it sunk down beneath the cold water.

It was late sun before we got it out. Granpa laid down on the bank and reached deep into the water and brought it up. He carried it, me and Granma following, to the shade of a great elm. There we sat around it in a circle, watching the cold water bead on the dark green skin. It was a ceremony.

Granpa pulled out his long knife and held it up. He looked at Granma and then at me, and laughed at my open mouth and big eyes watching; then he cut—the watermelon splitting ahead of the knife which means it is good. It was. When it was opened out, the juice made water balls on the red meat.

Granpa cut the slices. Granma and him laughed as the juice run down my mouth and over my shirt. It was my first watermelon.

Summer eased along. It was my season. My birthday being in the summer made it my season; that is the custom of the Cherokee. And so my birthday lasted, not a day, but a summertime.

It is the custom, during your season, to be told of your birthplace; of your father's doings; of your mother's love.

Granma said I was lucky, and more than likely one in a hundred million. She said I was born from nature—of Mon-a-lah—and so had all the brothers and sisters of which she had sung my first night in the mountains.

Granma said very few was picked to have the total love of the trees, the birds, the waters—the rain and the wind. She said as long as I lived I could always come home to them, where other children would find their parents gone and would feel lonesome; but I wouldn't ever be.

We sat on the back porch, in the dusk of summer evenings. The dark crept down the hollows while Granma talked soft. Sometimes she would pause and not go on for a long time, and then she would smooth her face with her hands and talk some more.

I told Granma I was right proud of the whole thing; and right off, I could tell that I wasn't afraid of dark in the hollows anymore.

Granpa said I had the uppers on him, being born special and all. He said he wished he had been picked out for such. Granpa said he had always been hampered with a suspicion of being frightened of the dark, and now would total depend on me to lead him about in dark situations. Which I told him I would.

Now I was six. Maybe it was my birthday that reminded Granma time was passing. She lit the lamp nearly every evening and read, and pushed me on my dictionary studying. I was down into the B's, and one of the pages was torn out. Granma said that page was not important, and the next time me and Granpa went to the settlement, he paid for and bought the dictionary from the library. It cost seventy-five cents.

Granpa didn't begrudge the money. He said he had always wanted that kind of dictionary. Since he couldn't read a word that was in it, I suspicioned that he had other using for it, but I never saw him touch it.

Pine Billy came by. He taken to coming more often after the watermelons ripened. Pine Billy liked watermelons. He wasn't uppity atall about the money he had got from the Red Eagle snuff company, nor the reward for the big-city criminals. He never mentioned it, so we never asked him about it.

Pine Billy said he figgered the world was coming to a end. He said all the signs pointed that way. He said there was rumors of wars, and famine had set on the land; banks was mostly closed and what wasn't closed was being robbed all the time. Pine Billy said there wasn't any money to be had hardly atall. He said that folks was still jumping out of winders in the big cities whenever the notion took them. Out in Oklahoma, he said, the wind was blowing away the ground.

We knew about that. Granma wrote to our kin in the Nations (we always called Oklahoma "the Nations" for that is what it was supposed to be, until it was taken from the Indians and made a state). They told us about it, in letters; how white men had turned grazing ground up with a plow, ground that was not supposed to be plowed. The wind was blowing it away.

Pine Billy said he determined to git saved since the end was near. He said fornicatin' had always been his biggest block toward gittin' saved. He said he fornicated at dances where he played, but he laid most of the faulting on the girls. He said they would not leave him alone. He said he had tried going to bush arbor meetings to git saved, but there was always girls around them too that kept after him to fornicate. He said he had found an old preacher who was too old to fornicate, he figgered, because he was holding a bush arbor meeting and was preaching, no-holds-barred, agin' fornicatin'.

Pine Billy said that this old preacher made you feel like, at the time, that you would totally give up fornicatin'. Pine Billy said that was what it took to save you—feeling that way at the time. He said he was going back and git saved—the world coming to an end, and all. Oncet you was saved, the primitive Baptists believed, you was always saved. If you backslid a little into *some* fornicatin', you was still saved, and more than likely had nothing to worry about.

Pine Billy said he leaned more toward the primitive Baptist as his religion. Which sounded reasonable to me.

Pine Billy played his fiddle in the dusk evenings of that summer. Could be it was because the world was coming to a end, but his music was sad.

It made you feel like this was the last summer; that you had already left it and wanted it back, and here you was all the time. You wisht he hadn't started playing, for you ached—and then you hoped he wouldn't stop. It was lonesome.

We went to church every Sunday. We walked the same trail that me and Granpa used to deliver our wares, for the church was a mile past the crossroads store.

We had to leave at daybreak, for it was a long walk. Granpa put on his black suit and the meal-sack shirt that Granma had bleached white. I had one too and wore clean overalls. Me and Granpa buttoned the top buttons on our shirts which made us proper for church.

Granpa wore his black shoes that he tallowed to shine. The shoes clumped when he walked. He was used to moccasins. I figured it was a painful walk for Granpa, but he never said anything, just clumped along.

Me and Granma had it easier. We wore moccasins. I was proud of how Granma looked. Every Sunday she wore a dress that was orange and gold and blue and red. It struck her at the ankles and mushroomed out around her. She looked like a spring flower floating down the trail.

If it hadn't been for the dress and Granma enjoying the outing so much, I suspicioned that Granpa would never have gone to church. Not counting the shoes, he never taken much to churching.

Granpa said the preacher and the deacons pretty much had a choke-hold on religion. He said they done the determining on who was going to hell and who wasn't, and if a feller didn't watch it, pretty soon he was worshiping the preacher and the deacons. So he said to hell with it. But he didn't complain.

I liked the walk to church. We didn't have to carry our load of wares, and as we walked the cutoff trail, day broke ahead of us. The sun hit the dew on the valley down below and made tree patterns where we walked.

The church set back off the road in a scope of trees. It was little and wasn't painted, but it was neat. Every Sunday, when we walked into the church clearing, Granma stopped to talk to some women; but me and Granpa headed straight for Willow John.

He always stood back in the trees, away from the people and the church. He was older than Granpa but he was as tall; full Cherokee with white plaited hair hanging below his shoulders, and a flat-brimmed hat pulled low to his eyes . . . like the eyes were private. When he looked at you, you knew why.

The eyes were black, open wounds; not angry wounds, but dead wounds that lay bare, without life. You couldn't tell if the eyes were dim, or if Willow John was looking past you into a dimness far away. Once, in later years, an Apache showed me a picture of an old man. It was Gokhla-yeh, Geronimo. He had the eyes of Willow John.

Willow John was over eighty. Granpa said that long ago, Willow John had gone to the Nations. He had walked the mountains, and would not ride in a car or train. He was gone three years and came back; but he would not talk of it. He would only say there was no Nation.

And so we always walked to him, standing back in the trees. Granpa and Willow John put their arms around each other and held each other for a long time; two tall, old men with big hats—and they didn't say anything. Then Granma would come, and Willow John would stoop and they would hold each other for a long time.

Willow John lived past the church, far back in the mountains; and so, the church being about halfway between us, it was the place they could meet.

Maybe children know. I told Willow John that there

was going to be lots of Cherokees before too long. I told him I was going to be a Cherokee; that Granma said I was natural-born to the mountains and had the feeling of the trees. Willow John touched my shoulder and his eyes showed a far back twinkle. Granma said it was the first time he had looked like that in many years.

We would not go into the church until everybody else was in. We always sat on the back row; Willow John, then Granma, me, and Granpa set next to the aisle. Granma held Willow John's·hand during church, and Granpa put his arm across the bench back and laid his hand on Granma's shoulder. I taken to holding Granma's other hand and putting a hand on Granpa's leg. This way I was not left out, though my feet always went to sleep as they stuck straight out over the seat rim.

Once, after we taken our seats, I found a long knife laying where I set. It was as long as Granpa's and had a deer skin sheath that was fringed. Granma said Willow John gave it to me. That is the way Indians give gifts. They do not present it unless they don't mean it and are doing it for a reason. They leave it for you to find. You would not get the gift if you didn't deserve it, and so it is foolish to thank somebody for something you deserve, or make a show of it. Which is reasonable.

I give Willow John a nickel and a bullfrog. The Sunday I brought it, Willow John had hung his coat on a tree while he waited for us, and so I slipped the bullfrog and the nickel into his pocket. It was a big bullfrog I had caught in the spring branch and had fed bugs until he was practical a giant.

Willow John put on his coat and went into church. The preacher called for everybody to bow their heads. It was quiet so that you could hear people breathing. The preacher said, "Lord . . ." and then the bullfrog said, "LARRRRRRRRUPP!" deep and loud. Everybody jumped and one man run out of the church. A feller hollered,

"God almighty!" and a woman screamed, "Praise the Lord!"

Willow John jumped too. He reached his hand in his pocket, but he didn't take out the frog. He looked over at me and the twinkle come again to his eyes; this time not so far back. Then he smiled! The smile broke across his face, wider and wider—and he laughed! A deep, booming laugh that made everybody look at him. He didn't pay any attention to them atall. I was scared, but I laughed too. Tears commenced to water in his eyes and roll down the creases and wrinkles of his face. Willow John cried.

Everybody got quiet. The preacher stood with his mouth open and watched. Willow John paid no attention to anybody. He didn't make a sound, but his chest heaved and his shoulders shook, and he cried a long time. People looked away, but Willow John and Granpa and Granma looked straight ahead.

The preacher had a hard time getting started again. He didn't mention the frog. He had tried once before to preach a sermon regarding Willow John, but Willow John never paid him any attention. He always looked straight before him, like the preacher wasn't there. The sermon had been on paying proper respect to the Lord's house. Willow John would not bow his head for prayers and he wouldn't take off his hat.

Granpa never commented on it. And so I thought on it, over the years. I figured it was Willow John's way of saying what he had to say. His people were broken and lost, scattered from these mountains that was their home and lived upon by the preacher and others there in the church. He couldn't fight, and so he wore his hat.

Maybe when the preacher said, "Lord . . ." and the frog said, "LARRRRRRRRUPP!" the frog was answering for Willow John. And so he cried. It broke some of the bitterness. After that, Willow John's eyes always twinkled and showed little black lights when he looked at me.

At the time I was sorry, but later I was glad I give Willow John the frog.

Every Sunday, after church, we went into the trees near the clearing and spread our dinner. Willow John always brought game in a sack. It would be quail, or venison, or fish. Granma brought corn bread and vegetable fixings. We ate there in the shade of big elms and talked.

Willow John would say the deer was moving farther back to high ground in the mountains. Granpa would say the fish baskets yielded such and so. Granma would tell Willow John to bring her his mending.

As the sun tilted and hazed the afternoon, we would get ready to leave. Granpa and Granma would each hug Willow John, and he would touch my shoulder with his hand, shy.

Then we would leave, walking across the clearing toward our cutoff trail. I would turn to watch Willow John. He never looked back. He walked, arms not swinging but straight by his sides, in a long, loping awkward step. Always looking to neither side; misplaced somehow—touching this fringe of the white man's civilization. He would disappear into the trees, following no trail that I could see, and I would hurry to catch up with Granpa and Granma. It was lonesome, walking the cutoff trail back home in the dusk of Sunday evenings, and we did not talk.

Will ye walk aways with me, Willow John? Not far;
A year or two, at ending of your time.
We'll not talk. Nor tell the bitter of the years.
Maybe laugh, occasional; or find a cause for tears;
Or something lost, could be, we both might find.

Will ye set a spell with me, Willow John? Not long;
A minute, measured by your length on earth.
We'll pass a look or two; we both will know
And understand the feeling; so when we go
We'll take comfort that we kin the other's worth.

Will ye linger at our leaving, Willow John? Just for me.
Lingering reassures and comforts us who part.
Memories of it help to slow the quickened tears
With recalling of you, in the later years;
And soften, some, the haunting of the heart.

Church-going

GRANPA SAID that preachers got so taken up with theirselves that they got the notion they personal held the door handle on the pearly gates and wouldn't let nobody in without their say-so. Granpa figgered the preachers thought God didn't have nothing atall to do with it.

He said a preacher had ought to work and git to know how hard a dollar was come by, then he wouldn't throw money around like its use was going to end tomorrow. Granpa said that good hard work whether it was in the whiskey trade or ever what would keep a preacher out of mischief. Which sounds reasonable.

People being so scattered, there was not enough to keep more than one church going. This led to some complications because there was so many different kinds of religion; folks believing so many different things that it made for disagreements.

There was hard-shell Baptists who believed that what was going to happen was going to happen and there was nothing you could do about it. There was Scot Presbyterians who would get stomping mad at such a notion. Each bunch could total prove out their viewpoint by the Bible. Which led to confusion as far as I was concerned as to what the Bible was talking about.

Primitive Baptists believed in taking up a "love offering" of money for the preacher and the hard-shells did not believe in paying a preacher anything. Granpa leaned toward the hard-shells on this point.

All the Baptists believed in baptizing, that is, getting total sunk under the waters in a creek. They said you could not be saved without it. The Methodists said that was wrong; that sprinkling on top of the head with water done the trick. They would each one whip out their Bibles there in the churchyard to prove out what they said.

It 'peared like the Bible told it both ways; but each time it told it, it cautioned you had better not do it the other way or you would go to hell. Or that's what they said it said.

One feller was of the Church of Christ. He said if you called the preacher "Reverend" that you would flat go to hell. He said you could call him "Mr." or "brother," but you had better not call him "Reverend." He had him a place in the Bible to prove it out; but a bunch of others proved out, also in the Bible, that you had *better* call him, "Reverend," or you would go to hell.

The Church of Christ feller was bad outnumbered and got hollered down, but he was stubborn and would not give it up. He made it a point to walk up to the preacher every Sunday morning and call him "Mr." This led to hard feelings between him and the preacher. Once they nearly come to blows in the churchyard but was separated.

I determined that I was not going to have anything atall to do with water around religion. And I was not going to call the preacher anything. I told Granpa it 'peared to be more than likely the safest thing to do, as you could easy git shipped down to hell depending on how the Bible was thinking at the time.

Granpa said if God was as narrer-headed as them idjits that done the arguin' about piddlin' such, then Heaven wouldn't be a fit place to live anyhow. Which sounds reasonable.

There was one family of Episcopalians. They was rich. They come to church in a car. It was the only car in the churchyard. The man was fat and wore a different suit might near every Sunday. The woman wore big hats; she was fat too. They had a little girl who always wore white dresses and little hats. She looked up all the time at something, though I could never determine what she was looking at. They always put a dollar in the collection plate. It was the only one in the plate every Sunday. The preacher met them at their car door and opened it for them. They set in the front row.

The preacher would be preaching. He would make a point, and look over at the front row and say, "Ain't that right, Mr. Johnson?" Mr. Johnson would give a little jerk of his head, certifying more or less that it was a fact. Everybody would look over to get Mr. Johnson's head jerk, and then settle back satisfied as it was so.

Granpa said he reckined Episcopalians had a total knowhow on the entire thing and didn't have to waller around on the fringes worrying about water and such. He said they *knowed* where they was going and was closemouthed about letting anybody else git in on it.

The preacher was a skinny man. He wore the same black suit every Sunday. His hair stuck out on all sides and he had the appearance of being nervous all the time. Which he was.

He was friendly to folks in the churchyard, though I never went up to him; but when he got in total control, standing in the pulpit, he got mean. Granpa said this was because he knowed it was agin' the rules for anybody to jump up and challenge him while he was preaching.

He never said anything about water, which was disappointin'. I was interested in finding out the way you had better not use it. But he laid it heavy on the Pharisees. He would get to working up on the Pharisees and come down out of the pulpit and run up the aisle toward us.

Sometimes he would might near lose his breath, he got so mad at them.

One time he was giving the Pharisees hell and had come down the aisle. He would holler about them and suck in his breath so hard his throat would rattle. He run down close to where we was setting, and pointed his finger at me and Granpa and said, "You *know* what they was up to. . . ." It 'peared like he was accusing me and Granpa of having something to do with the Pharisees. Granpa set up in his seat and give the preacher a hard look. Willow John looked toward him and Granma held his arm. The preacher turned off to pointing at somebody else.

Granpa said he had never knowed any Pharisees and was not going to have any son of a bitch accusing him of having knowledge of nothing they had done. Granpa said the preacher had better commence to point his finger some'eres else. Which after that he did. I reckined he saw the look in Granpa's eye. Willow John said the preacher was crazy and would bear close watching. Willow John always carried a long knife.

The preacher also had a total disliking for Philistines. He was continually raking them up one side and down the other. He said they was, more or less, as low-down as Pharisees. Which Mr. Johnson nodded his head that it was so.

Granpa said he got tired of hearing the preacher raking somebody over *all* the time. He said he didn't see any earthly reason for gittin' the Pharisees and Philistines stirred up; there was enough trouble as it was.

Granpa always put something in the collection plate, though he disagreed with paying preachers. He said it paid the rent on our bench, he reckined. Sometimes he give me a nickel that I could put in. Granma never put anything in and Willow John would not look at the collection plate when they passed it.

Granpa said if they kept continually sticking the collection plate under Willow John's nose, that Willow John would take something *out* of it; figuring they was continually offering him some of it.

Once a month there was testifying time. This is when people would stand up, one by one, and tell how much they loved the Lord, and what all bad they had done. Granpa would never do it. He said all it done was cause trouble. He said he knew personal of several men who had been shot afterward when they had told something they had done to a feller, and the feller hadn't knowed about it until he heard tell of it from the church. Granpa said such wasn't any business but his own. Granma and Willow John didn't stand up.

I told Granpa I felt more or less like he did about it and was not going to stand up either.

One man said he was saved. He said he was going to stop liquorin' up; said he had been liquorin' around fairly heavy for a number of years and now was not going to do it anymore. Which made everybody feel good; him trying to better himself. People shouted, "Praise the Lord!" and "Amen!"

Every time somebody got up and started telling the bad things he had done, a man over in a corner would always holler, "Tell it all! Tell it all!" He would keep this up every time it 'peared they was going to stop, and they would try to think of something else bad they had done. Sometimes they come out with some pretty bad things, which they might not have done if the man had not been hollering. He never did stand up.

One time a woman stood up. She said the Lord had saved her from wicked ways. The man in the corner hollered, "Tell it all!"

Her face turned red, and she said she had been fornicatin'. She said she was going to stop. She said it was not right. The man hollered, "Tell it all!" She said she had done some fornicatin' with Mr. Smith. There was a commotion while Mr. Smith disassociated hisself from the bench he was on and come walking down the aisle. He walked real fast and went out the church door. About that time two fellers on a back bench got up and eased out the door without hardly any commotion atall.

She called out two more names with which she had done some fornicatin'. Everybody was praising her and telling her she had done right.

When we left the church house, the men all walked wide around the woman and would not speak to her. Granpa said they was scared to be seen talking to her. Some of the womenfolks, however, crowded around her and beat her on the back and patted her and told her she had done the right thing.

Granpa said these was women who was wanting to know about their own menfolks, and they figgered if they showed how comforting it was to talk and how good you got treated by talking, they could git some more fornicatin' women to testify.

Granpa said if they did, it would be a hell of a mess. Which it would.

Granpa said he hoped the woman didn't change her mind and decide to go back to fornicatin'. He said she would be in for a disappointment. He said she would not find anybody hardly atall to fornicate with, less'n he was drunk and out of his senses.

Every Sunday before preaching started there was a special time set aside when anybody could stand up and tell about folks who needed help. Sometimes it would be a sharecropper between movings who didn't have anything to eat for his family, or somebody whose house had burned down.

All the people in the church would bring things to help. We always carried a lot of vegetables in the summertime, which we had plenty of. In the winter we would carry meat. One time Granpa made a hickory limb chair and seated it with stripped deer hide for a family that had lost their furniture in a fire. Granpa taken the man aside there in the churchyard and give him the chair and spent a long time showing him how to make it.

Granpa said if you showed a feller how to do, it was a lot better than giving him something. He said if you learnt a man to make for hisself, then he would be all right; but if you just give him something and didn't learn him anything, then you would be continually giving to the man the rest of your natural life. Granpa said you would be doing the man a disservice, for if he become dependent on you, then you taken away his character and had stole it from him.

Granpa said some folks liked to just continually give because it made them feel uppity, and better than the feller they was giving to; when all they had to do was learn the feller a little something which would make him dependent on hisself.

Granpa said human nature being what it was they was some fellers found out that some people liked to feel uppity. He said these fellers got to be such sorry men that they was anybody's dog that would hunt them. They got down to where they would rather be a hound to Mr. Uppitys than to be their own man. He said they continually whined about what they needed, when what they needed was some learning done by a hard boot stuck in their backside.

Granpa said some nations was uppity in the same way and would give and give so they could call theirselves big shots, when if they had their heart in the right place, would learn the people to who they was giving how to do for theirselves. Granpa said these nations wouldn't do this because then the other people would not be dependent on them, and that's what they was after in the first place.

Me and Granpa was creek washing when he got to talking about it. He got worked up on the whole thing and we had to crawl out on the bank, or he would, more than likely, have drowned in the waters. I asked Granpa who Moses was.

Granpa said he had never got a right clear picture of Moses, what with the preacher a'suckin' air and rattling and hollering. The preacher said Moses was a disciple.

Granpa cautioned me not to take his word as bound oath, because he couldn't tell me anything except what he had *heard* about Moses.

He said Moses taken up with a girl in some bull rush reeds, which he understood growed on the riverbank. He said this was natural, but the girl was rich, and as a matter of fact belonged to a mean son of a bitch called Faro. He said Faro was always killing people. Faro got it in for Moses, more than likely on account of the girl. Which causes some trouble today.

Granpa said Moses hid out and taken the people with him that Faro was trying to kill. He said Moses headed out into a country that didn't have any water in it; and Moses taken a stick and hit a rock and some water come out of it. Granpa said he had no notion atall how he done it . . . but that is what he heard.

Granpa said Moses wandered around for years with no idee whatsoever as to where he was going. As a matter of fact, he never did git there but the people that kept follering him around did git there. Wherever it was they was going. He said Moses died while he was still wandering around.

Granpa said Samson come in there somewheres and killed a lot of Philistines who was always making trouble. He said he didn't know what the fight was about, or if the Philistines was Faro's men or not.

Granpa said a conniving woman got Samson drunk and cut his hair off. He said the woman fixed Samson so his enemies could git at him. Granpa couldn't recollect the woman's name, but he said it was a good Bible lesson;

that you was to watch out for conniving women who tried to git ye drunk. Which I said I would.

Granpa taken great satisfaction from learning me that Bible lesson. It was, more than likely, the only one he had ever learnt anybody.

Looking back on it, me and Granpa was pretty ignorant of the Bible. And I guess, confused as to all the technical ways by which you got to Heaven. Me and Granpa more or less figgered we was out of the whole thing, technical wise, for we never could get it reasoned out to make any sense atall.

Once you give up on something, then you are kind of an onlooker. Me and Granpa was onlookers when it come to technical church religion, and had no anxious feeling about it atall . . . as we had give it up.

Granpa said I had just as well fergit about the water situation. He said he had totally give up on it a long time ago, and felt better since that time.

He said he, privately speaking, couldn't reason as to what in the hell water had to do with it.

I felt the same way and so give up on the water.

Mr. Wine

HE HAD COME all through the winter and the spring, once a month, regular as sundown, and spent the night. Sometimes he would stay over with us a day and another night. Mr. Wine was a back peddler.

He lived in the settlement, but walked the mountain trails with his pack on his back. We always knew about the day he would come, and so when the hounds bayed me and Granpa would go down the hollow trail to meet him. We would help him carry his pack to the cabin.

Granpa would carry the pack. Mr. Wine usually had a clock with him that he let me carry. He worked on clocks. We didn't have one, but we helped him work on his clocks on the kitchen table.

Granma would light the lamp and Mr. Wine would put a clock on the table and open its insides. I was not tall enough to see by setting down, so I always stood on a chair next to Mr. Wine and watched him take out little springs and gold screws. Granpa and Mr. Wine talked while he worked on the clocks.

Mr. Wine was maybe a hundred years old. He had a long white beard and wore a black coat. He had a little round black cap that set on the back of his head. Mr. Wine was not his real name. His name started off with Wine, but it was so long and complicated we couldn't get it straight, so we called him Mr. Wine. Mr. Wine said it didn't matter. He said names was not important, it was more or less how you said it. Which is right. Mr. Wine said some Indian names was beyond anything atall that he could say proper so he made up names hisself.

He always had something in his coat pocket; usually an apple, one time he had an orange. But he could not remember anything.

We would eat supper in dusk evening; then, while Granma cleared the table, Mr. Wine and Granpa would set in rockers and talk. I would pull my chair between them and set too. Mr. Wine would be talking and stop. He would say, "It seems like I'm forgetting something, but I don't know what it is." I knew what it was, but would not say anything. Mr. Wine would scratch his head and comb his beard with his fingers. Granpa wouldn't help atall. Finally Mr. Wine would look down at me and say, "Could you help me remember what it is, Little Tree?"

I would tell him, "Yes, sir, more than likely, you was totin' something in your pocket that you couldn't recollect."

Mr. Wine would jump straight up in his chair and slap at his pocket and say, "Whangdaggle me! Thank you Little Tree, for reminding me. I'm gettin' so I can't think." Which he was.

He would pull out a red apple that was bigger than any kind raised in the mountains. He said he run acrost it and picked it up, and was intending to throw it away, as he didn't like apples. I always told him I would take it off his hands. I stood ready to split with Granma and Granpa, but they didn't like apples either. Which I did. I saved the seeds and planted them along the spring branch, intending to raise lots of trees that give up that kind of apple.

He could not remember where he put his glasses. When he worked on the clocks, he wore little glasses on the end of his nose. They were held together with wire and the handles that went behind his ears had cloth wrapped around them.

He would stop working and push his glasses up on his head while he talked to Granpa. When he started back to work, he couldn't find them. I knew where they was. He would feel around on the table and look at Granpa and Granma, and say, "Now where in devil's torment is my glasses?" Him and Granpa and Granma would all grin at each other, feeling foolish that they didn't know. I would point to his head and Mr. Wine would slap hisself on the head, total stumped that he had left them there.

Mr. Wine said he could not work on his clocks if I had not been there to help him find his glasses. Which he couldn't.

He learnt me to tell time. He would twist the hands of the clock around and ask me what time it was, and would laugh when I missed. It didn't take me long before I knew everything.

Mr. Wine said I was getting a good education. He said there wasn't hardly any young'uns atall my age that knew about Mr. Macbeth or Mr. Napoleon, or that studied dictionaries. He learnt me figures.

I could already figure money somewhat, being in the whiskey trade, but Mr. Wine would take out some paper and a little pencil and put figures down. He would show me how to make the figures and how to add them, and take away, and multiply. Granpa said I was might near better than anybody he had ever seen, doing figures.

Mr. Wine gave me a pencil. It was long and yeller. There was a certain way you sharpened it, so that you didn't make the point too thin. If you made the point too thin it would break, and you would have to sharpen it again; which used up the pencil for no need atall.

Mr. Wine said the way he showed me how to sharpen the pencil was the thrifty way. He said there was a difference between being stingy and being thrifty. If you was stingy, you was as bad as some big shots which worshiped money and you would not use your money for what you had ought. He said if you was that way then money was your god, and no good would come of the whole thing.

He said if you was thrifty, you used your money for what you had ought but you was not loose with it. Mr. Wine said that one habit led to another habit, and if they was bad habits, it would give you a bad character. If you was loose with your money, then you would get loose with your time, loose with your thinking and practical everything else. If a whole people got loose, then politicians seen they could get control. They would take over loose people and before long you had a dictator. Mr. Wine said no thrifty people was ever taken over by a dictator. Which is right.

He had the same consideration as me and Granpa for politicians.

Granma usually bought some thread from Mr. Wine. Little spools of thread was two for a nickel and there was big spools that was a nickel apiece. Sometimes she bought buttons, and once she bought some red cloth with flowers on it.

There was all kinds of things in the pack; ribbons of every color, pretty cloth and stockings, thimbles and needles, and little shiny tools. I would squat by the pack when Mr. Wine opened it on the floor and he would hold up things and tell me what they was. He give me a figuring book.

The book had all the figuring in it, and told you how to do it. This was so I could learn to do figuring all through the month. I got so far ahead each month that when Mr. Wine come by, he was total stumped.

Mr. Wine said figuring was important. He said education was a two-part proposition. One part was technical, which was how you moved ahead in your trade. He said he was for getting more modern in that end of education. But, he said, the other part you had better stick to and not change it. He called it valuing.

Mr. Wine said if you learnt to place a value on being honest and thrifty, on doing your best, and on caring for folks; this was more important than anything. He said if you was not taught these values, then no matter how modern you got about the technical part, you was not going to get anywheres atall.

As a matter of fact, the more modern you got without these valuings, then you would more than likely use the modern things for bad and destroying and ruining. Which is right, and not long after that was proved out.

Every once in a while we had a hard time fixing the clocks, so Mr. Wine would stay with us a day and another night. Once he brought a black box with him which he said was a Kodak. He could take pictures with it. He said he was not very good at it—taking the pictures. He said some folks had ordered the Kodak and he was taking it to them, but he said it would not hurt it atall or show any use if he taken our picture.

He taken a picture of me, and of Granpa too. The box would not take the picture unless you was facing d'rect at the sun, and Mr. Wine said he was not too took up with the whole contraption anyhow. Granpa wasn't either. He was suspicious of the thing and would not stand but for one picture. Granpa said you never knowed about them things and it was best not to use anything new like that until you found out what would happen over a period of time.

Mr. Wine wanted Granpa to take a picture of me and him. It took us practical all evening to take it. Me and Mr. Wine would get all set. He would have his hand on my head, and we would both be grinning at the box. Granpa would say he couldn't see us through the little hole. Mr. Wine would go to Granpa and get the box leveled up and come back. We would stand again. Granpa would say we would have to move over a ways, as he couldn't see anything but an arm.

Granpa was nervous about the box. I suspicioned he figured they was something in it that was liable to get out. Me and Mr. Wine faced the sun so long that neither one of us could see a thing before Granpa finally got the picture taken. It didn't work out though. The next month when Mr. Wine brought the pictures, mine and Granpa's showed up plain, but me and Mr. Wine was not even in the picture that Granpa had taken. We could make out the tops of some trees and some specks above the trees; which after studying the picture awhile Granpa said was birds.

Granpa was proud of the bird picture and I was too. He taken it to the crossroads store and showed it to Mr. Jenkins, and told him he had personally taken the picture of the birds.

Mr. Jenkins couldn't see good. Me and Granpa worked at it for might near an hour, pointing out the birds; and he finally saw them. I figured me and Mr. Wine was more than likely standing somewhere down below the birds.

Granma would not have her picture taken. She would not say why, but she was suspicious of the box and would not touch it.

After we got the pictures back, Granma was taken with them. She studied them a lot and put them on the log over the fireplace, and was continually watching them. I believe she would have stood for a picture after that; but we didn't have the Kodak, as Mr. Wine had to deliver it to the people who had ordered it.

Mr. Wine said he was going to get another Kodak but he didn't for this was his last summer.

Summer was getting ready to die, dozing away the days at the ending. The sun commenced to change from the white heat of life to a hazing of yeller and gold, blurring the afternoons and helping summer die. Getting ready, Granma said, for the big sleep.

Mr. Wine made his last trip. We didn't know it then, though me and Granpa had to help him across the foot log and up the steps of the porch. Maybe he knew.

When he unstrapped his pack, there on the cabin floor, he taken out a yeller coat. He held it up and the lamp shined on it like gold. Granma said it reminded her of wild canaries. It was the prettiest coat we had ever seen. Mr. Wine turned it round and round in the lamp light and we all looked at it. Granma touched it, but I didn't.

Mr. Wine said he didn't have any sense and was always forgetting things, which he was. He said he had made the coat for one of his great-grand young'uns which lived acrost the big waters, but he made the size for what his great-grand young'un was years ago. After he got it made, then he remembered that it was a total misfit. Now there wasn't anybody could wear it.

Mr. Wine said it was a sin to throw something away that could be used by somebody. He said he was so worried that he couldn't sleep, because he was getting old and couldn't stand any more sin put on him. He said if he couldn't find somebody which would favor him by wearing the coat that he reckined he was total lost. We all studied on that for a while.

Mr. Wine had his head bowed and looked like he was done lost already. I told him I would try to wear it.

Mr. Wine looked up and his face broke out in a grin amongst the whiskers. He said he was so forgetful he had plumb forgot to ask me for the favor. He pulled hisself up and danced a little jig around and said I had totally lifted a sin and a big load off of him. Which I had.

Everybody put the coat on me. Granma pulled on the sleeve, while I stood there with it on. Mr. Wine smoothed the back and Granpa pulled the bottom down. It fit perfect; as I was the same size as Mr. Wine had remembered his great-grand young'un.

I turned round and round in the light, for Granma to see all sides. I held out my arms so Granpa could see the sleeves, and we all felt of it. It was soft and slid smooth and easy under our hands. Mr. Wine was so happy that he cried.

I wore my coat when we et supper and was careful to keep my mouth over the plate and not spill anything on it. I would have slept in it, but Granma said sleeping in it would make it wrinkle. She hung it on the post of my bed so I could look at it. The moonlight coming through my winder made it shine even more.

Laying there, looking at the coat, I determined right off that I would wear it to church and to the settlement. I might even wear it to the crossroads store when we delivered our wares. It 'peared to me that the more I wore it, the more sin would get lifted off Mr. Wine.

Mr. Wine slept on a pallet quilt. He laid it out on the floor of the settin' room, across the dogtrot from our sleeping rooms. I told him he could use my bed, as I liked to sleep on a pallet, but he would not do it.

That night, as I lay abed, some how or other I got to thinking that even though I was doing Mr. Wine a favor, maybe I'd ought to thank him for the yeller coat. I got up and tiptoed across the dogtrot and eased open the door. Mr. Wine was kneeling on his pallet and had his head bowed. He was saying prayers, I figured.

He was giving thanks for a little boy who had brought him so much happiness; which I figured was his great-gran young'un acrost the big waters. He had a candle lit on the kitchen table. I stood quiet, for Granma had learnt me not to make a noise while people was saying prayers.

In a minute, Mr. Wine looked up and saw me. He told me to come in. I asked him why he had lit the candle, when we had a lamp.

Mr. Wine said all his folks was acrost the big waters. He said there was not but one way he could be with them. He said he only lit the candle at certain times, and they lit a candle at the same time, and that they was together when they did this for their thoughts was together. Which sounds reasonable.

I told him we had folks scattered far off in the Nations, and had not figured such a way as that to be with them. I told him about Willow John.

I said I was going to tell Willow John about the candle. Mr. Wine said Willow John would understand. I plumb forgot to thank Mr. Wine for the yeller coat.

He left the next morning. We helped him acrost the foot log. Granpa had cut a hickory stick and Mr. Wine used it as he walked.

He went down the trail, hobbling slow, using the hickory stick and bent under the weight of his pack. He was out of sight when I remembered I had forgot. I run down the trail, but he was far below me, picking his way along. I hollered, "Thankee for the yeller coat, Mr. Wine." He didn't turn and so did not hear me. Mr. Wine was not only bad about forgettin'; he couldn't hear good either. I figured, coming back up the trail, that him always forgettin' he would understand how I forgot too.

Even though I was doing him a favor—wearing the yeller coat.

Down from the Mountain

FALL CAME EARLY to the mountains that year. First, along the rims high against the sky, the red and yellow leaves shook in a brisking wind. Frost had touched them. The sun turned amber and slanted rays through the trees and into the hollow.

Each morning, the frost worked its way farther down the mountain. A timid frost, not killing, but letting you know that you couldn't hold onto summer no more than you could hold back time; letting you know that the winter dying was coming.

Fall is nature's grace time; giving you a chance to put things in order, for the dying. And so, when you put things in order, you sort out all you must do . . . and all you have not done. It is a time for remembering . . . and regretting, and wishing you had done some things you have not done . . . and said some things you had not said.

I wished I had thanked Mr. Wine for the yeller coat. He didn't come that month. We set on the porch in late evenings and watched the hollow trail, and listened; but he didn't come. Me and Granpa determined we would go to the settlement to see about him.

Frost touched the hollow; light, barely reminding. It

turned the persimmon red and ran yellow trimmings around the edges of the poplar and maple leaves. The creatures who was to stay the winter worked harder putting up their stores so not to die.

Blue jays made long lines, flying back and forth to the high oaks, carrying acorns to their nests. Now they didn't play or call.

The last butterfly flew up the hollow. He rested on a cornstalk where me and Granpa had stripped the corn. He didn't flex his wings, just set, and waited. He had no purpose in storing food. He was going to die, and he knew it. Granpa said he was wiser than a lot of people. He didn't fret about it. He knew he had served his purpose, and now his purpose was to die. So he waited there in the last warm of the sun.

Me and Granpa got in stove wood and fireplace logs. Granpa said we had grasshoppered around all summer and now was pushed to get our winter's warm settled up. Which we had.

We dragged dead tree trunks and heavy limbs from the mountainside into the clearing. Granpa's axe flashed in the evening sun and rang and echoed up the hollow. I toted in the wood chips for the kitchen bin and racked the fireplace logs against the cabin side.

This is what we was doing when the politicians came. They said they was not politicians, but they was. A man and a woman.

They would not take the rockers offered to them, but set straight in the high back chairs. The man wore a gray suit and the woman wore a gray dress. The dress was choked so tight around her neck that I figured it made her look the way she did. The man held his knees together like a woman. He kept his hat on his knees and was nervous, for he continually turned the hat round and round. The woman wasn't nervous.

The woman said that I had ought to leave the room, but

Granpa said that I set in on everything there was to set in on. So I stayed and set in my little rocker and rocked.

The man cleared his throat and said people was concerned about my education and such. He said that it had ought to be looked after. Granpa said it was. He told them what Mr. Wine said.

The woman asked Granpa who Mr. Wine was, and he told her all about Mr. Wine—though he didn't mention how Mr. Wine was always fergittin' everything. The woman sniffed her nose and brushed around at her skirts like she figured Mr. Wine was somewheres about and fixing to get under her dress.

I seen right off she total discounted Mr. Wine; which she did us too. She give Granpa a paper which he give to Granma.

Granma lit the lamp and set at the kitchen table to read the paper. She started to read it out loud but she stopped. She read the rest of it to herself. When she finished she stood up and leaned over—and blew out the lamp.

The politicians knew what this meant. I did too. They stood up in the half light and stumbled out the door. They didn't say good-bye.

We waited in the dark, a long time after they they left. Granma lit the lamp and we set at the kitchen table. I couldn't see what was on the paper, as my head only come above the table edge, but I listened.

The paper said some people had filed with the law. It said I was not being done right by. The paper said Granma and Granpa had no right to keep me; that they was old and had no education. It said Granma was a Indian and Granpa was a half-breed. Granpa, it said, had a bad reputation.

The paper said Granma and Granpa was selfish, and being that way was total hampering me for the rest of my continual life. They was selfish, it said, because they just wanted comfort in their old age and was putting me out, more or less, to give it to them.

The paper had things to say about me, but Granpa would not read it out loud. It said that Granpa and Granma had so many days in which they could come in court and give answer to it. It said otherwise I was to be put in a orphanage.

Granpa was total stumped. He taken off his hat and laid it on the table, and his hand shook. He rubbed his hat with his hand and just set, looking at the hat and rubbing it.

I went and set in my rocker by the fireplace and rocked. I told Granma and Granpa that I figgered I could up my dictionary learning to practically ten words a week. I told them that more than likely I could up it even more— maybe to a hundred. I was learning to read, and I told them I seen right off that I was going to have to double up on my reading, and I reminded them what Mr. Wine had said about my figgering; which, even though he didn't count none with the politicians, it still showed I was moving ahead.

I couldn't stop talking. I tried to stop, but I couldn't. I rocked harder and harder, and talked faster and faster.

I told Granpa I was in no wise hampered atall; that I figgered I was gittin' the uppers on just about everything. Granpa would not answer me. Granma held the paper and stared at it.

I seen they figgered they was what the paper said they was. I said they wasn't. I said it was the other way around; that they comforted me, and I was more than likely about the worst thing that had come along for them to have to mind about. I told Granpa I had burdened them up pretty heavy and they had not, in no wise, burdened me. I told them I stood ready to tell the law this very thing. But they wouldn't talk.

I said I was gittin' ahead otherwise too, learning a trade

and all. I told Granpa that I was total certain no other young'un my age was learning a trade.

Granpa looked at me for the first time. His eyes was dull. He said maybe, the law being like they was, that we had ought not to mention about the trade.

I went to the table and set on Granpa's leg. I told him and Granma I would not go with the law. I said I would go back in the mountains and stay with Willow John, until such time as the law forgot about the whole thing. I asked Granma what a orphanage was.

Granma looked at me across the table. Her eyes didn't look right either. Granma said a orphanage was where they kept young'uns who didn't have a Pa and a Ma. She said they was lots of young'uns there. She said the law woud come looking if I went back and stayed with Willow John.

I seen right off that the law might find our still if they taken to looking. I didn't mention Willow John again.

Granpa said we would go to the settlement in the morning and see Mr. Wine.

We left at daybreak, down the hollow trail. Granpa had the paper to show Mr. Wine. Granpa knew where he lived, and when we got to the settlement we turned down a side street. Mr. Wine lived over a feed store. We went up long ladder steps, that wobbled as we climbed up the side of the feed store. The door was locked. Granpa shook it and knocked on it . . . but nobody answered. There was dust over the glass and Granpa wiped it away and looked in. He said there wasn't anything in there.

We walked slow back down the steps. I followed Granpa around to the front of the feed store, and we went in.

Coming out of the noontime sun, it was dark in the store. Me and Granpa stood for a minute to get our sight. A man was leaning against the counter.

"Howdy," he said, "what fer ye?" His stomach hung over the belt of his britches.

"Howdy," Granpa said, "we was looking for Mr. Wine, the feller which lives over yer store."

"Mr. Wine ain't his name," the man said. He had a toothpick in his mouth which he worked from side to side. He sucked on the toothpick and taken it out and frowned at it, like it tasted bad.

"In fact," he said, "he ain't got *no* name no more. He's dead."

Me and Granpa was stumped. We didn't say anything. I felt hollow inside and my knees weakened. I had built up a pretty heavy dependence on Mr. Wine as handling our situation. I figured Granpa had counted heavy on it too; for he didn't know what to do next.

"Yer name be Wales?" the fat man asked.

"It be," Granpa said. The fat man walked behind the counter, reached under it and dragged out a tow sack. He swung it up on the counter. It was full of something.

"The old man left this here fer ye," he said. "See, the tag. Got yer name on it." Granpa looked at the tag, though he couldn't read it.

"He had everything tagged," the fat man said. "Knew he was going to die. Even had a tag tied around his wrist telling where to ship the body. Knew exactly how much it cost too . . . left the money in an envelope . . . right down to the penny. Stingy. No money left over. Just like a damn Jew."

Granpa looked up, hard, from under his hat. "Paid his obligations, didn't he?"

The fat man got serious. "Oh yes . . . yes . . . I had nothin' against the old man, didn't know him. Nobody much did. Spent all his time wandering around in the mountains."

Granpa swung the tow sack over his shoulder. "Could ye d'rect me to a lawyering man?" The fat man pointed across the street. "Right in front of ye, up the stairs, 'tween them buildings."

"Thankee," Granpa said. We walked to the door.

"Funny thing," the fat man said after us, "the old Jew, when we found him; the only thing he hadn't tagged was a candle. The dern fool had it lit and burning right beside him."

I knew about the candle, but I didn't say anything. I knew about the money too. Mr. Wine was not stingy; he was thrifty, and paid his obligations, and seen that his money was used in the right manner.

We went across the street and up the steps. Granpa toted the sack. Granpa knocked on a door that had glass across the top and lettering on it.

"Come in . . . come in!" The voice sounded like you wasn't supposed to knock. We went in.

A man was leaning back in a chair, behind a desk. He had white hair and looked old. When he saw me and Granpa he got up, slow. Granpa taken off his hat and set down the tow sack. The man leaned over his desk and stuck out his hand. "My name is Taylor," he said, "Joe Taylor."

"Wales," Granpa said. Granpa taken his hand, but didn't shake it. He turned loose of it and handed Mr. Taylor our paper.

Mr. Taylor set down and taken eyeglasses out of a vest pocket. He leaned on the desk and read the paper. I watched him. He frowned. He looked at the paper for a long time.

When he finished, he folded the paper slow and handed it back to Granpa. He looked up. "You've been in jail— whiskey-making?"

"Oncet," Granpa said.

Mr. Taylor got up and walked to a big window. He looked down in the street a long time. He sighed; and didn't look at Granpa. "I could take your money, but it wouldn't do any good. Government bureaucrats that run these things don't understand mountain people. Don't want

to. I don't think the sons of bitches understand anything."
He was looking a long way off at something out the
window. He coughed. "Nor Indians. We'd lose. They'll
take the boy."

Granpa put on his hat. He taken his purse from his
forward pants pocket and unsnapped and felt around. He
laid a dollar on Mr. Taylor's desk. We left. Mr. Taylor
was still looking out the window.

We walked out of the settlement, Granpa leading, totin'
the tow sack. Mr. Wine was gone. I knew we had lost.

It was the first time I could keep up, easy, with Granpa.
He walked slow. His moccasins dragged in the dirt. I
figured he was tired. We was on the hollow trail when I
asked him, "Granpa, what is a damn Jew?"

Granpa stopped and didn't look back at me. His voice
sounded tired too. "I don't know; something is said about
'em in the Bible, somewhere's or other; must go back a
long ways." Granpa turned around. "Like the Indian . . .
I hear tell they ain't got no nation, neither." Granpa looked
down at me. His eyes looked like Willow John's.

Granma lit the lamp. We opened the tow sack there on
the kitchen table. There was rolls of red cloth and green
and yeller cloth for Granma; needles, thimbles and spools
of thread. I told Granma it looked like Mr. Wine had
might near emptied his pack into the tow sack. She said
it looked that way to her.

There was all manner of tools for Granpa And books.
A figuring book and a little black book that Granma said
had valuing sayings in it for me. There was a book with
pictures of boys and girls and dogs. It had writing in it
and was brand-new, for it still shined. I figured Mr.
Wine was going to bring it on his next trip, if he didn't
forget. That was all; we thought.

Granpa picked up the empty sack and started to put it
on the floor. Something bumped in the sack. Granpa
turned it up. A red apple rolled out on the table. It was

the first time that Mr. Wine had recollected the apple.
Something else rolled out and Granma picked it up. It was
a candle and it had one of Mr. Wine's tags on it. Granma
read it. It said: Willow John.

We didn't eat much supper. Granpa told about our
trip to the settlement; about Mr. Wine and what Mr.
Taylor had said.

Granma blew out the lamp and we set by the fireplace
in the half dark of a new moon coming through the
winder. We didn't light a fire. I rocked.

I told Granma and Granpa they was not to feel bad
about it. I said I didn't. More than likely I would like the
orphanage, with all the young'uns and such being there.
I said it would not take long to satisfy the law, more than
likely, and I could come back.

Granma said we had three days, and then I was to be
delivered up to the law. We didn't talk anymore. I didn't
know what to say. We all three rocked, our chairs creak-
ing slow, far into the night and we didn't talk.

When we went to bed, for the first time since Ma died
I cried, but I put the blanket in my mouth and Granma
and Granpa did not hear me.

We filled up the three days, living hard as we could.
Granma went everywhere with me and Granpa, up the
Narrows to Hangin' Gap. We taken Blue Boy and the
hounds. One morning, early in the dark, we taken the high
trail. We set on top of the mountain and watched day break
over the rims. I showed Granpa and Granma my secret
place.

Granma spilt sugar in practical everything she cooked.
Me and Granpa eat fairly heavy on meal cookies.

The day before I was to leave, I slipped off over the
cutoff trail to the crossroads store. Mr. Jenkins said the
red and green box was old, and so he would sell it for
sixty-five cents, which I paid him. I bought a box of
red stick candy for Granpa, which cost a quarter. This left
me a dime out of the dollar I had got from Mr. Chunk.

That night Granpa cut my hair. He said it was necessary, for it might be hard on me, looking like a Indian and all. I told Granpa I didn't care. I said I had just as soon look like Willow John.

I was not to wear my moccasins. Granpa stretched my old shoes. He taken a piece of iron and pushed it into the shoes, punching the leather of the uppers out over the soles. My feet had growed.

I told Granma I would leave my moccasins under my bed, as I would more than likely be back pretty soon, and they would be handy. I put my deer shirt on the bed. I told Granma that it could stay there as nobody would be sleeping in my bed until I come back.

I hid the red and green box in Granma's meal bin where she would find it in a day or two; and put the box of stick candy in Granpa's suit coat. He would find it Sunday. I had only taken out one piece to more or less prove it out. It was good.

Granma would not go to the settlement for the leaving. Granpa waited in the clearing for me, and Granma knelt down on the porch and held me like she held Willow John. I held her too. I tried not to cry, but I did, some. I had on my old shoes, which if I stretched my toes, they didn't hurt. I wore my best overalls and my white shirt. I wore the yeller coat. In my tow sack, Granma had put two more shirts and my other pair of overalls, and my socks. I would not carry anything else, for I knew I would be back. I told Granma I would.

Kneeling there on the porch, Granma said, "Do ye recollect the Dog Star, Little Tree? The one we look at in the dusk of evening?" I said I did. And Granma said, "Wherever ye are—no matter where—in the dusk of evening, ye look at the Dog Star. Me and Granpa will be looking too. We will remember." I told her I would remember too. It was like Mr. Wine and his candle. I asked Granma to tell Willow John to look at the Dog Star too. Which she said she would.

Granma held me by the shoulders and looked at me. She said, "The Cherokees married your Pa and Ma. Will ye remember that, Little Tree? No matter what is said . . . remember."

I said I would. Granma turned me loose. I picked up my tow sack and followed Granpa out of the clearing. Across the foot log, I looked back. Granma was standing on the porch, watching. She raised her hand and touched her heart, and pushed the hand after me. I knew what she meant.

Granpa had on his black suit. He had his shoes on too, and we both kind of clumped along. Down the hollow trail, pine branches swept low and held my arms. An oak limb reached out fingers and pulled the tow sack off my shoulder. A persimmon bush grabbed my leg. The spring branch commenced to run harder and jump and fuss, and a crow flew down across us and cawed over and over . . . and then set on a high tree top and cawed and cawed. All of them was saying, "Don't go, Little Tree . . . don't go, Little Tree. . . ." I knew what they was saying. And so my eyes blinded and I stumbled along behind Granpa. The wind rose and moaned and picked at the tail of my yeller coat. Dying briers reached over the trail path and hung theirselves on my legs. A mourning dove called, long and lonesome—and was not answered, so I knew she was calling for me.

Me and Granpa had a hard time making it down the hollow trail.

We waited in the bus station; me and Granpa setting on a bench. I held my tow sack in my lap. We was waiting for the law.

I told Granpa I didn't hardly see how he was going to make it in the whiskey trade, me not being there to help. Granpa said it would be hard. He would have to double up on his work time. I told Granpa that more than likely I would be back pretty quick, and he wouldn't have to double up long. Granpa said more than likely I would. We didn't say much else.

A clock ticked on the wall. I could tell the time, and I told Granpa. There wasn't many people in the bus station. A woman and a man. Times being hard, Granpa said, folks wasn't traveling by paying ways. Which they wasn't.

I asked Granpa, reckin if the mountains run down as far as the orphanage. Granpa said he didn't know. He had not been there. We waited some more.

The woman came in. I knew her; it was the woman in the gray dress. She come up to me and Granpa, and when Granpa stood up, she handed him some papers. Granpa put them in his pocket. She said the bus was waiting. She said, "We don't want any fuss now. Let's get on with it. What has to be done, has to be done; best for everybody."

Which I didn't know what she was talking about. Granpa didn't either. She was all business. She taken a string out of her purse and tied it around my neck. It had a tag on it, like one of Mr. Wine's tags. The tag had writing on it. Me and Granpa followed her out the back of the bus station to the bus.

I had my tow sack throwed over my shoulder. Granpa knelt there, by the open door of the bus, and held me like he held Willow John. He held me a long time, kneeling on the pavement with both his knees. I whispered to Granpa. I said, "I'll more than likely be back, d'rectly." Granpa squeezed me that he heard.

The woman said, "You'll have to go now." I didn't know whether she was talking to me or Granpa. Granpa stood up. He turned and walked off and he didn't look back.

The woman picked me up and set me on the step of the bus, which I could have made it myself. She told the bus driver to read my tag, and so I stood for him while he read it.

I told the bus driver I didn't have a ticket and wasn't

right sure about riding as I didn't have any money. He laughed and said the woman had give him my ticket. There wasn't but three people on the bus. I went back and set down by a winder where maybe I could see Granpa.

The bus started up and moved out of the station. I saw the woman with the gray dress watching. We moved down the street and I couldn't find Granpa anywhere. Then I saw him. He was standing on the corner of the street by the bus station. He had his hat pulled down low and his hands hung down by his sides.

We went by him and I tried to raise the winder, but I didn't know how. I waved, but he didn't see me.

As the bus passed on, I run to the back of the bus and looked out the back winder. Granpa was still there, watching the bus. I waved and hollered, "Good-bye Granpa. I'll be back more than likely pretty quick." He didn't see me. I hollered some more. "I'll more than likely be back d'rectly, Granpa." But he just stood. Getting smaller and smaller in the late evening sun. His shoulders sloped. Granpa looked old.

The Dog Star

WHEN YOU DON'T know how far you are going, it is far away. Nobody had told me. I reckin Granpa didn't know.

I couldn't see over the backs of the seats in front of me, and so I watched out the winder; the houses and trees going by, and then just trees. It got dark and I couldn't see anything.

I peeped around the seat up the aisle, and saw the road ahead shining in the bus lights. It all looked the same way.

We stopped at a bus station in a town and stayed a long time, but I didn't get off or move from my seat. I figgered more than likely I was safer where I was.

After we left the town, there was nothing else to watch. I kept my tow sack in my lap, for it felt like Granpa and Granma. It smelled kind of like Blue Boy. I dozed off.

The bus driver wakened me. It was morning and drizzling rain. We had stopped in front of the orphanage and when I got off the bus a white-headed lady was waiting under an umbrella.

She had on a black dress that come to the ground and she looked like the lady in the gray dress, but she wasn't.

She didn't say anything. She bent and taken hold of my
tag and read it. She nodded to the bus driver and he
closed his door and left. She straightened up and frowned
a minute and sighed. "Follow me," she said, and led the
way, walking slow, through iron gates. I put my tow sack
over my shoulder and followed her.

We went through the gates with big elms on each side
which rustled and talked as we passed. The lady taken
no notice whatsoever, but I did. They had heard about
me.

We walked across a big yard toward some buildings. I
could keep up easy. When we got to the door of a building, the lady stopped. "You are going to see the Reverend,"
she said. "Be quiet, don't cry and be respectful. You can
talk, but *only* when he asks a question. Do you understand?" Which I told her I did.

I follered her down a dark hall and we went into a
a room. The Reverend was sittin' at a desk. He didn't
look up. The lady set me down in a straight chair in front
of his desk. She tiptoed out of the room. I put my tow
sack in my lap.

The Reverend was busy, reading papers. He had a pink
face which looked like he washed it fairly heavy, for it
shined. He didn't have any hair to speak of, though I seen
some around his ears.

There was a clock on the wall, and I told the time. I
didn't say it out loud. I could see rain running down the
winder in back of the Reverend. The Reverend looked up.

"Stop swinging your legs," he said. He said it right
hard. Which I did.

He studied some more at the papers. He laid the papers
down and taken up a pencil which he turned end over
end in his hands. He put his elbows on the desk and leaned
over as I didn't come up very high for him to see.

"These are hard times," he said. He frowned like he was
personal settin' on the hard times. "The State hasn't the

money for these matters. Our Denomination has agreed
to take you—possibly against our better judgment, but we
have."

I commenced to feel right bad about the Denomination
having to mess with the whole thing. I didn't say anything,
as he had not asked me a question.

He turned the pencil over and over again; which was
not sharpened thrifty, for the point was too thin. I suspicioned he was looser than he put hisself up to being. He
commenced again. "We have a school you can attend. You
will be assigned small work details. Everybody here does
some work; something you are probably not accustomed
to. You must follow the rules. If you break them, you will
he punished." He coughed. "We have no Indians here,
half-breed or otherwise. Also, your mother and father were
not married. You are the first, the only bastard we have
ever accepted."

I told him what Granma had said; that the Cherokees
married my Pa and my Ma. He said what Cherokees done
didn't count none whatsoever. He said he had not asked me
a question. Which he hadn't.

He commenced to get worked up about the whole
thing. He stood up and said his Denomination believed in
being kind to everybody; kind to animals and such.

He said I did not have to go to the church services
and the evening chapels; as bastards, according to the
Bible, could not be saved. He said I *could* go to listen in
on it more or less, if I was quiet and set in the back and
taken no part whatsoever.

Which I didn't mind, as me and Granpa had already
give up, technical-wise, on the entire thing.

He said he seen by the papers on his desk that Granpa
was not fittin' to raise a young'un, and that I more than
likely had not ever had any discipline. Which I hadn't, I
don't reckin. He said Granpa had been in jail.

I told him I might near got hung oncet myself. He

stopped with his pencil in the air and his mouth opened. "You *what?*" He hollered.

I said I might near got hung by the law oncet; but I got away. I told him if it hadn't been for the hound dogs, I reckin I would have got hung. I didn't tell him where the still was; as this might lead to puttin' me and Granpa out of the whiskey trade.

He set down at his desk and put his face in his hands, like he was crying. He shook his head back and forth. "I *knew* this was the wrong thing to do," he said. He said it two or three times. Which I wasn't sure which thing was wrong he was talking about.

He set so long shaking his head in his hands that I suspicioned he was crying. I commenced to feel might near as bad as him about the whole thing, and was sorry I had brought up about might near being hung. We set like this awhile.

I told him not to cry. I told him I was not hurt in anyway atall and was not nor ever had got worked up about it. I told him however, that ol' Ringer died. Which was my fault.

He raised up his head and said, "Shut up! I have not asked you a question!" Which he hadn't. He taken up his papers. "We'll see . . . we'll try, with the Lord's help. It may be that you belong in a reform school," he said.

He rung a little bell on his desk and the lady come jumping in the room. She had stood outside all the time, I reckined.

She told me to foller her. I taken up my tow sack and put it over my shoulder and said, "Thankee," but I didn't say Reverend. Even if I was a bastard and going to hell, I was not in any ways figgering to go any faster, since it hadn't been settled whether you was to call such "Reverend" or "Mister." Like Granpa said, if you was not pushed, there was not any sense atall running unnecessary chances.

The wind rose up as we left the room and splattered

the winder hard. The lady stopped and looked. The
Reverend turned and looked at the winder too. I knew
word had come about me, from the mountains.

My cot set in a corner. It was separate from the others
except for one, which was pretty close to me. It was a
big room and had twenty or thirty boys who stayed there.
Most of them was older than me.

My job was to help sweep up the room every morning
and every evening. I done it easy; but when I didn't sweep
under the cots good enough, the lady made me do it over
again. Which happened fairly regular.

Wilburn slept on the cot that was closest to mine. He
was a lot older than I was; maybe eleven. He said he was
twelve. He was tall and skinny and had freckles all over
his face. He said he would not ever get adopted by anybody and would have to stay there until he was might near
eighteen. Wilburn said he didn't give a damn. He said
when he got out, he was going to come back and burn the
orphanage down.

Wilburn had a clubfoot. It was his right foot and turned
plumb inwards, making the toes of his high foot scrape
his left leg when he walked and the right side of him kind
of jumped along.

Me and Wilburn didn't play in any of the games in the
yard. Wilburn couldn't run, and I reckin I was too little
and didn't know how to play. Wilburn said he didn't give a
damn. He said games was for babies. Which is right.

Me and Wilburn set under a big oak in the corner of
the yard during playtime. Sometimes when the ball come
far out in the yard, I would run and get it and throw
it back to the boys who was playing the game. I could
throw good.

I talked to the oak tree. Wilburn didn't know it, for I
didn't use words. She was old. With winter coming on,
she had lost most of her talking leaves, but she used her
naked fingers in the wind.

She said she was getting sleepy, but was going to stay awake to send back to the mountain trees that I was here. She said she would send it on the wind. I told her to tell Willow John, which she said she would do.

I found a blue marble under the tree. You could see all the way through it and when you held it up to one eye and shut the other one, everything looked blue. Wilburn told me what it was, for I had not seen a marble.

He said you wasn't supposed to look through marbles, was supposed to thump them on the ground; but if I thumped mine, somebody would take it away from me, as somebody had lost it.

Wilburn said, finders keepers, losers weepers; and they could go to hell. I put the marble in my tow sack.

Every oncet in a while, all the boys lined up in the hall by the office and men and ladies come by and looked at them. They was looking for somebody to adopt. The white-headed lady in charge of us said I was not to line up. Which I didn't.

I watched them from the door. You could tell who got picked. They would stop in front of the one they wanted and talk to him; and they would all go into the office. Nobody ever talked to Wilburn.

Wilburn said he didn't give a damn, but he did. Every time it was line-up day, Wilburn put on a clean shirt and overalls. I watched Wilburn.

When he was in line, he always grinned at everybody that come by and taken his clubfoot and hid it behind his other leg. But they wouldn't talk to him. Every night after line-up day, Wilburn peed on his cot. He said he done it deliberate. He said he done it to show them what he thought of their damn adopting.

Whenever Wilburn peed on his cot, the white-headed lady would make him take his mattress and blankets outside the next day and lay them in the sun. Wilburn said he didn't care. He said if they messed with him much, he was going to pee on his cot every night.

Wilburn asked me what I was going to do when I growed up. I told him I was going to be a Indian like Granpa and Willow John and live in the mountains. Wilburn said he was going to rob banks and orphanages. He said he would rob churches too, if he could find out where they kept their money. He said, more than likely, he would kill everybody that run banks and orphanages, but he would not kill me.

Wilburn cried at night. I never let on I knew, for he stuck his blanket in his mouth, which I figgered he didn't want anybody to know. I told Wilburn he could more than likely get his foot fixed straight when he got out of the orphanage. I give him my blue marble.

Chapel services was held at dusk evening, just before supper time. I didn't go, and skipped supper too. This give me a chance to watch the Dog Star. There was a winder halfway down the room from my cot, and from it I could see the Dog Star real plain. It rose in the dusk with a bare twinkle and got brighter as night darkened.

I knew Granma and Granpa was watching it, and Willow John. I stayed by the winder every evening for an hour and watched the Dog Star. I told Wilburn if he wanted to skip supper some night, he could watch it with me, but they made him go to chapel and he wouldn't give up supper. He never watched it.

At first when I commenced to watch it I tried to think up things during the day that I would remember that night, but I found out that this was not necessary.

All I had to do was watch. Granpa sent me remembrance of me and him settin' on top of the mountain, watching the day birthing, with the sun hitting the ice and sparkling. I heard him plain as speaking, "She's coming alive!" And there by the winder, I would say, "Yes, sir, she's coming alive!"

Me and Granpa went back fox huntin' watching the Dog Star; with Blue Boy and Little Red, and ol' Rippitt and Maud. We laughed might near until we couldn't stand it at ol' Rippitt.

Granma sent remembrances of the root gathering and the times she spilt sugar in the acorn meal. And the time she caught me and Granpa on our hands and knees in the corn patch, braying like a mule at ol' Sam.

She sent me a picture of my secret place. The leaves was all fallen, brown and rust and yeller on the ground. Red sumach hemmed it like a ring of fire torches that would not let anybody in but me.

Willow John sent me pictures of the deer in the high ground. Me and Willow John laughed about the time I put the frog in his coat pocket. Willow John's pictures would get fuzzy, for his feeling was strong on something. Willow John was mad.

Every day I watched the clouds and the sun. If it was cloudy, I would not be able to watch the Dog Star. When this happened, I stood by the winder and listened to the wind.

I was put in a grade of school. We done figgering which I already knew; for Mr. Wine had taught me. A big fat lady headed up the learning. She meant business and would not tolerate any foolishness atall.

One time she held up a picture that showed a deer herd coming out of a spring branch. They was jumping on one another and it looked like they was pushing to get out of the water. She asked if anybody knew what they was doing.

One boy said they was running from something, more than likely a hunter. Another boy said they didn't like water and was hurrying to get across. She said this was right. I raised my hand.

I said I seen right off they was mating; for it was buck deer that was jumping the does; also, I could tell by the bushes and trees that it was the time of the year when they done their mating.

The fat lady was total stumped. She opened her mouth,

but didn't say anything. Somebody laughed. She slapped
her hand on her for'ad and walled her eyes back and
dropped the picture. I see right off she was sick.

She staggered back'ards a step or two before she got
aholt of her total senses. Then she run at me. Everybody
got quiet. She grabbed me by the neck and commenced
to shake me. Her face got red and she commenced to
holler, "I should have *known*—we *all* should have known
. . . filth . . . filth . . . would come out of you . . . you . . .
little *bastard*!"

I hadn't no way in the world of knowing what she was
hollering about, and stood ready to set it right. She shaken
me some more and then clasped her hand behind my neck
and pushed me out of the room.

We went down the hall to the Reverend's office. She
made me wait outside and shut the door behind her. I
could hear them talking, but could not understand what
they was saying.

In a few minutes she come out of the Reverend's office
and walked off down the hall without looking at me. The
Reverend was standing in the door. He said, real quiet,
"Come in." I went in.

His lips was parted like he was going to grin, but he
wasn't. He kept running his tongue over his lips. There
was sweat on his face. He told me to take off my shirt.
Which I did.

I had to pull my overall galluses off my shoulders, and
when I got my shirt off, this made me have to hold up my
overalls with both hands. The Reverend reached behind
his desk and taken up a long stick.

He said, "You are born of evil, so I know repentance is
not in you; but praise God, you are going to be taught not
to inflict your evil upon Christians. You can't repent . . .
but you shall cry out!"

He cut loose with the big stick acrost my back. The
first time it hurt; but I didn't cry. Granma had learnt me.
Oncet when I stumped off my toenail . . . she learnt me

how the Indian bears pain. He lets his body mind go to sleep, and with his spirit mind, he moves out of his body and *sees* the pain—instead of *feeling* the pain.

The body mind only feels body pain. The spirit mind only feels spirit pain. So I let my body mind sleep.

The stick splattered and splattered acrost my back. After a while it broke. The Reverend got another stick. He was panting hard; "Evil is stubborn," he said while he was panting. "But praise God, right will prevail."

He kept swinging his new stick until I fell down. I was wobbly but I got up. Granpa said if ye could stay on yer feet, more than likely, ye would be all right.

The floor tilted a little, but I seen right off I could make it. The Reverend was out of breath. He told me to put my shirt on. Which I did.

The shirt soaked up some of the blood. Most of the blood had run down my legs into my shoes, as I didn't have any underwearing to catch it. This made my feet sticky.

The Reverend said I was to go back to my cot and I was not to eat supper for a week. Which I didn't eat supper anyway. He said I was not to go back to the grade or leave the room for a week neither.

It felt better not to use my galluses, so that evening at dusk, I held up my overalls when I stood by the winder and watched the Dog Star.

I told Granpa and Granma and Willow John about it. I told them I had no way in the world of knowing how I made the lady sick; nor what come over the Reverend. I told them I stood ready to make amend, but the Reverend said I couldn't, as I was born evil and would not know how.

I told Granpa that it 'peared to me that more than likely I couldn't hardly no way atall handle the situation. I said I wanted to come home.

It was the first time I ever went to sleep watching the Dog Star. Wilburn wakened me under the winder when he got back from supper. He said he left supper early so as to see about me. I slept on my stomach.

Wilburn said when he growed up and left the orphanage and taken to robbing orphanages and banks and such, that he would kill the Reverend right off. He said he didn't care if he *did* go to hell, like I was.

Every evening after that, when dusk brought the Dog Star up, I told Granma and Granpa and Willow John I wanted to come home. I would not see the pictures they sent, nor listen. I told them I wanted to come home. The Dog Star turned red and whitened and turned red again.

Three nights later, the Dog Star was hid by heavy clouds. Wind tore down a light pole and the orphanage was dark. I knew they had heard.

I commenced to expect them. Winter come on. The wind sharpened and cried around the building at night. Some didn't like it, but I did.

Outside now, I spent all my time under the oak tree. She was supposed to be asleep, but she said she wasn't, on account of me. She talked slow—and low.

Late one evening, just before we was to go in, I thought I seen Granpa. It was a tall man and he wore a big black hat. He was moving away from me down the street. I run to the iron fence and I hollered, "Granpa! "Granpa!" He didn't turn.

I run down the fence as far as it went and he was disappearing. I hollered loud as I could, "Granpa! It's me, Little Tree!" But he didn't hear, and was gone.

The white-headed lady said Christmas was might near on us. She said everybody was to be happy and sing. Wilburn said they sung all kind of songs in the chapel. He said they had to learn the songs and the pets got to stand up around the Reverend like chickens with white sheets on and bellered at the songs. I could hear them.

The white-headed lady said Sandy Claws was coming. Wilburn said that was a pile of shit.

Two men brought in a tree. They had on suits like

politicians. They laughed and grinned and said, "Looky here, boys, what we have brought you. Isn't that nice? Now isn't that nice? You have your very own Christmas tree!"

The white-headed lady said it was real nice and she told everybody to tell the two politicians it was real nice and to thank them. Which everybody did.

I didn't. There was no cause atall to cut the tree. It was a male pine and it died slow, there in the hall.

The politicians looked at their watches and said they couldn't stay long, but they wanted everybody to be happy. They said they wanted everybody to take some red paper and put it on the tree. Everybody did except me and Wilburn.

The politicians left and hollered, "Merry Christmas!" when they went out the door. We all stood around and looked at the tree for a while.

The white-headed lady said that tomorrow was Christmas Eve and that Sandy Claws would come with presents about noontime. Wilburn said, "Ain't that a funny time for Sandy Claws to be coming on Christmas Eve?" The white-headed lady frowned at Wilburn. She said, "Now Wilburn, you say that every year. You know very well that Sandy Claws has got to go a lot of places. You also know that he and his helpers have a right to be home with their families on Christmas Eve. You should be thankful they take the time—anytime—to come and give you Christmas."

Wilburn said, "Bullshit."

Sure enough, the next day four or five cars come up to the door. Men and ladies got out and had packages in their arms. They had on funny little hats and some of them had little bells in their hands. They rung the bells and hollered. "Merry Christmas!" They hollered this over and over. They said they was Sandy Claws' helpers. Sandy Claws come in last.

He had on a red suit and had pillers stuffed under his

belt. His beard was not real, like Mr. Wine's; it was tied
on and hung limp below his mouth. It didn't move when
he talked. He hollered, "Ho! Ho! Ho!" He kept hollering
this over and over.

The white-headed lady said we was all to be happy and
holler back "Merry Christmas!" at them. Which everybody did.

A lady give me a orange, which I thanked her for it.
She kept standing over me and saying, "Don't you want to
eat the nice orange?" So I et it while she watched me. It
was good. I thanked her again. I told her it was a good
orange. She asked me if I wanted another one. I told her
I reckined. She went off somewheres and never did get another one. Wilburn got a apple. It was not as big as the
ones Mr. Wine was always fergittin' he had in his pocket.

I wisht then that I had saved a piece of my orange,
which I would have if the lady hadn't been pushing me to
eat it. I would have traded some of it for some of Wilburn's
apple. I was partial towards apples.

The ladies all commenced ringing their bells and hollering, "Sandy Claws is going to give out the gifts! Gather
round in a circle! Sandy Claws has something for you!" We
all gathered round in a circle.

When Sandy Claws called out your name, you had to
step forward and get your gift from him. Then you was to
stand while he patted you on the head and rubbed your
hair. Then you thanked him for it.

One of the ladies would be right on you hollering, "Open
up your gift! Aren't you going to open up the nice gift?"
Which got confusing, the more was given out; as ladies
was running this away and that away trying to foller everybody around.

I got my gift, and thanked Sandy Claws. He rubbed me
on the head and said, "Ho! Ho! Ho!" A lady commenced
hollering at me to open it up; which I was trying to do.
I finally got the wrapping off.

It was a cardboard box with the picture of a animal

on it. Wilburn said it was the picture of a lion. The box had a hole in it, and you was supposed to pull a string through the hole, and it would sound like a lion, Wilburn said.

The string was broke, but I fixed it. I tied a knot in it. The knot would not come through the hole, which made the lion not growl much. I told Wilburn it sounded more like a frog to me.

Wilburn got a water pistol; but it leaked. He tried to shoot with it, but the water kind of angled down. Wilburn said he could pee farther than that. I told Wilburn we could more than likely fix it if we had some sweet gum; but I didn't know where there was a sweet gum tree thereabouts.

A lady come by passing out a piece of stick candy to everybody. I got one. She bumped into me again and give me another piece. I split the extry with Wilburn.

Sandy Claws started hollering, "Good-bye everybody! See you next year! Have a Merry Chrismas!" All the men and ladies started hollering the same thing and ringing their bells.

They went out the front door and got in their cars and taken off. Everything seemed quiet after that. Me and Wilburn set on the floor by our cots.

Wilburn said the men and ladies come out of a chamber in town and a country club. He said they come out every year so they could feel good when they went and got drunk. Wilburn said he was tired of the whole thing. He said when he got out of the orphanage, he was not never going to pay any attention to Christmas, whatsoever.

Just as dusk begun to fall, they all had to go to the chapel for Christmas Eve. I stayed by myself, and as it got darker, I could hear them singing. I stood by the winder. The air was clear and the wind was still. They sung about a star, but it wasn't the Dog Star, for I listened close. I watched the Dog Star rising bright.

They stayed a long time, singing in the chapel, so I

got to watch the Dog Star until it rose high. I told Granma and Granpa and Willow John I wanted to come home.

Christmas Day we had a big dinner. Each one of us got a chicken leg and either a neck or a gizzard. Wilburn said it was always that-a-away. He said he figured they raised special chickens that didn't have nothing but legs, necks and gizzards. I liked mine and et it all.

After dinner we could do as we pleased. It was cold outside and everybody stayed in except me. I went acrost the yard and carried my cardboard box and set under the oak tree. I set a long time.

It was nearly time for dusk and me to go in, when I looked up toward the building.

There was Granpa! He was coming out of the office and walking toward me. I dropped my cardboard box and run at him, hard as I could. Granpa knelt and we held each other and did not speak.

It was getting dark and I couldn't see Granpa's face under the big hat. He said he had come to see about me, but had to go back home. He said Granma couldn't come.

I wanted to go—worst I ever felt—but I was afraid it would cause Granpa trouble. So I didn't say I wanted to go home. I walked with him to the gate. We held one another again, but Granpa walked off. He walked slow.

I stood there a minute, watching him go away in the dark. The thought come to me that more than likely, Granpa might have trouble finding the bus station. I follered along though I didn't know where the bus station was myself, but I might be able to help.

We walked down a road, me follering behind, and then onto some streets. I saw Granpa cross a street and come up behind the bus station. There was lights where he was standing. I hung around the corner where I was.

It was quiet, being Christmas Day and practical nobody was about. I waited awhile and then I hollered. "Granpa, more than likely I could help ye with the bus lettering."

Granpa didn't act stumped atall. He waved for me to come on over. I ran. We stood at the back of the station, but I couldn't make out which lettering was which.

In a little while a loudspeaker told Granpa which one was his bus. I walked over to the bus with him. The door was open and we stood there a minute. Granpa was looking off somewheres. I pulled on his pants leg. I didn't hold on like I had done after Ma's funeral, but I kind of pulled. Granpa looked down. I said, "Granpa. I want to go home."

Granpa looked at me a long time. He reached down and swung me up in his arms and set me on top of the bus step. He come up to the step and taken out his snap purse. "I'm paying for myself and my young'un," Granpa said, and he said it hard. The bus driver looked at him, and he didn't laugh.

Me and Granpa walked to the back of the bus. I was hoping the bus driver would hurry and close the door. Eventually he did, and we started up, leaving the bus station behind.

Granpa reached his arm around me and lifted me onto his lap. I laid my head on his chest, but I didn't sleep. I watched the winder. It was frosted with ice. There wasn't any heat there in the back of the bus, but we didn't care.

Me and Granpa was going home.

See the mountains humping and rolling high
Rimming the day birth and busting the sun
And tucking the fog sheets 'round her knees
And strumming the wind with her finger-trees
And scratching her back against the sky.

Watch the cloud banks roll and stroke her hips
Dripping whispers of sighs from the branch and bush
Hear her womb-hollows stir with the murmur of life
Feel the warm of her body, the sweet of her breath
And the rhythm of mating that thunders and cries.

Deep in her belly the water veins pulse
And nipple the roots that suckle their life
And streams from her breasts in a liquid flow
Giving life to her children she cradles in love
And adding a lilt from Her spirit mind
The melody humming of water's song.

Me and Granpa's going home.

Home Again

WE RODE THE hours away. Me and Granpa, my head
on his chest and not talking, but not sleeping either. The
bus stopped two or three times at bus stations, but me
and Granpa stayed on. Maybe we was afraid something
would happen to hold us back.

It was early morning, but still dark when me and Granpa
got off the bus on the side of the road. It was cold and
there was ice on the ground.

We set out up the road and after a while we turned
up the wagon ruts. I saw the mountains. They loomed big
and darker than the dark around us. I might near broke
into a run.

By the time we turned off the wagon ruts onto the
hollow trail, the dark was fading into gray. I told Granpa,
of a sudden, that something was wrong.

He stopped. "What is it, Little Tree?"

I set down and pulled off my shoes. "I reckined I
couldn't feel the trail, Granpa," I said. The ground felt
warm and run up through my legs and over my body.
Granpa laughed. He set down too. He pulled off his shoes
and stuffed his socks in them. Then he stood up and
throwed the shoes back toward the road as far as he could
throw them.

"And ye can have them clobbers," Granpa hollered! I throwed mine back toward the road and hollered the same thing; and me and Granpa commenced to laugh. We laughed 'til I fell down and Granpa was might near rolling on the ground hisself and tears was running down his face.

We didn't know exactly what we was laughing at, but it was funnier than anything we had laughed at before. I told Granpa if folks could see us, they would say we was white whiskey drunk. Granpa said he reckined . . . but maybe we *was drunk*—in a way.

As we come up the trail, the first pink touched the east rim. It got warm. Pine boughs swept down over the trail and felt my face and run theirselves over me. Granpa said they was wanting to make sure it was me.

I heard the spring branch and it was humming. I run and laid down and turned my face to the water while Granpa waited. The spring branch slapped me light, and run over my head and felt for me—and sung louder and louder.

It was good light when we saw the foot log. The wind had picked up. Granpa said it wasn't moaning nor sighing, it was singing in the pines and would tell everything in the mountains that I was home. Ol' Maud bayed.

Granpa hollered, "Shut up, Maud!" And here come the hounds acrost the foot log.

They all hit me at oncet and knocked me down. They licked me all over the face and every time I tried to get up one of them jumped on my back and there I went again.

Little Red commenced to show out by jumping all four feet in the air and twisting at the top of his jump. He would yelp as he leaped. Maud commenced doing it, and ol' Rippitt tried it and tumbled in the spring branch.

Me and Granpa was hollering and laughing and slapping at hounds as we come to the foot log. I looked to the porch, but Granma wasn't there.

I was halfway acrost the foot log and got scared, for I couldn't see her. Something told me to turn around. There she was.

It was cold, but she only had on a deerskin dress and her hair shined in the morning sun. She stood on the side of the mountain beneath the bare branches of a white oak. She was watching like she wanted to look at me and Granpa without being seen.

I hollered, "Granma!" And fell off the foot log. It didn't hurt. I splashed in the water and it was warm against the morning chill.

Granpa leaped in the air and spraddled out his legs. He hollered, "Whooooooooeeeeeeee!" and hit the water. Granma run down the mountain. She run into the spring branch and dived at me, and we rolled, splashing and hollering and crying some, I reckin.

Granpa was settin' in the spring branch and throwing water up in the air. The hounds all stood on the foot log and looked at us, total stumped at the whole thing. They figgered we was crazy, Granpa said. They jumped in too.

A crow commenced to caw, settin' high atop a pine. He swooped low over us, cawing, and headed up the hollow. Granma said he was going to tell everybody I was home.

Granma hung my yeller coat by the fireplace to dry. I had had it on when Granpa come to the orphanage. I went into my room and put on my deer shirt and britches . . . and my boot moccasins.

I run out the door and up the hollow trail. The hounds went with me. I looked back and saw Granpa and Granma standing on the back porch watching. Granpa was still barefooted and he had his arm around Granma. I run.

Ol' Sam snorted when I passed the barn and trotted after me aways. Up the hollow trail, and the Narrows— all the way to Hangin' Gap, I didn't want to stop running. The wind sung along with me and squirrels and 'coons and birds come out on tree limbs to watch and holler at me as I passed. It was a bright winter morning.

I come back slow down the trail and found my secret place. It was just like the picture Granma had sent me. Rust leaves was deep over the ground, under bare trees, and red sumach closed in where nobody could see. I laid on the ground a long time and talked to the sleepy trees, and listened to the wind.

The pines whispered and the wind picked up, and they commenced to sing, "Little Tree is home . . . Little Tree is home! Listen to our song! Little Tree is with us! Little Tree is home!" They hummed it low and sung it higher, and the spring branch sung it too along with them. The hounds noticed, for they quit sniffing the ground and stood with their ears up and listened. The hounds knew and come closer around me and laid down, content with the feeling.

Through that short winter day, I lay in my secret place. And my spirit didn't hurt anymore. I was washed clean by the feeling song of the wind and the trees and the spring branch and the birds.

They didn't care or understand how the body minds worked, no more than the men of body minds understood or cared for them. So they did not tell me about hell, or ask me where I come from, or say anything about evil atall. They didn't know such word-feelings; and in a little while I had forgot them too.

When the sun had set behind the rim and shafted its last light through Hangin' Gap, me and the hounds walked back down the hollow trail.

As the hollow softened blue, I saw Granma and Granpa settin' on the back porch, facing up the hollow toward me, waiting, and as I come to the back porch, they stooped and we held on to one another. We didn't need words, and so did not say them. We knew. I was home.

When I pulled off my shirt that night, Granma saw the

whip scars and asked me. I told her and Granpa, but I said it didn't hurt.

Granpa said he would tell the high sheriff and that nobody was to come for me again. I knew when Granpa set his mind and said it—then they would not come. Granpa said it would be best not to tell Willow John of the whipping. Which I said I wouldn't.

By the fireplace that night, Granpa told it. How they commenced to have bad feelings, watching the Dog Star, and then one evening at dusk Willow John was standing at the door.

He had walked to the cabin through the mountains. He didn't say anything, but et supper with them by the light of the fire. They didn't light the lamp and Willow John did not pull off his hat. He slept in my bed that night, but when they got up in the morning, Granpa said, Willow John was gone.

That Sunday when him and Granma went to church Willow John was not there. On a branch of the big elm, where we always met, Granpa found a message belt. It said Willow John would be back and that all was well. The next Sunday it was still there; but the Sunday after that Willow John was waiting for them. He didn't say where he had been, so Granpa didn't ask.

Granpa said the high sheriff sent him word that he was wanted at the orphanage, and he went. He said the Reverend looked sick and said he was signing give-up papers on me. He said he had been followed around for two days by a savage, and that the savage had eventually come into his office and said that Little Tree was to come home to the mountains. That was all the savage said, and walked off. The Reverend said he did not want any trouble with savages and pagans and such.

I knew then who it was I had seen walking away down the road that I had thought was Granpa.

Granpa said when he come out of the office and seen me,

he knew at the time I was to be given up; but he didn't know if I was more taken with being around young'uns . . . or wanted to come home . . . so he let me decide.

I told Granpa I seen right off what I wanted to do the minute I got to the orphanage.

I told Granma and Granpa about Wilburn. I left my cardboard box under the oak tree and I knew Wilburn would find it. Granma said she would send Wilburn a deer shirt. Which she did.

Granpa said he would send him a long knife, but I told Granpa more than likely Wilburn would stab the Reverend with it. Granpa didn't send it. We never heard nothing more of Wilburn.

When we went to church that Sunday, I was first across the clearing. I run way ahead of Granma and Granpa. Willow John was standing back in the trees, where I knew he would be; the old straight-brimmed black hat settin' on top of his head. I run as hard as I could and grabbed Willow John around the legs and hugged him. I said, "Thankee, Willow John." He didn't say anything but reached and touched my shoulder. When I looked up, his eyes was twinkling and shining, black deep.

The Passing Song

WE WINTERED GOOD; though me and Granpa was put to it to keep up with the wood cutting. Granpa had got behind and said that if I had not come back, they would more than likely have froze that winter. Which they would.

It was a hard freeze winter. We most times had to set fires and thaw out our running lines at the still, when we run off our wares.

Granpa said hard winters was necessary occasional. It was nature's way of cleaning things up and making things grow better. The ice broke off the weak limbs of the trees, so only the strong ones come through. It cleaned out the soft acorns and chinkapins, chestnuts and walnuts, and made for a hardier food crop in the mountains.

Spring come, and planting time. We upped our corn planting, figuring to make the run of our wares a little bigger in the fall.

It was hard times, and Mr. Jenkins said the whiskey trade was picking up while everything else was going down. He said he reckined a feller had to drink more whiskey to fergit how bad off he was.

During the summer I come up to seven years. Granma

give me the marriage stick of my Ma and Pa. It didn't have many notches on it, for they was not married long. I put it in my room across the headboard of my bed.

Summer give way to fall, and one Sunday, Willow John didn't come. We come across the clearing that Sunday but we didn't see him standing under the elm. I run far back into the trees and called, "Willow John!" He was not there. We turned back and didn't go to church. We come home.

Granma and Granpa was worried about it. I was too. He had left no sign, for we looked. Granpa said something was wrong. Me and Granpa determined to go and find him.

We set out before day, that Monday morning. By early light we was past the crossroads store and the church. After that, we commenced to walk might near straight upward.

It was the highest mountain I had ever walked. Granpa had to slow down and I kept up easy. It was an old trail, so dim you almost couldn't see it, running along a ridge that sloped upward and onto another mountain. The trail sidled up the mountain, but always it went up.

The trees was shorter and more weathered. At the top of the mountain a little fold run into the side; not deep enough to be called a hollow. Trees grew on its sides and pine needles carpeted the floor. Willow John's lodge was there.

It was not built of big logs, like our cabin, but of smaller lodge poles and set back in the trees against the bank of the fold, sheltered.

We had brought Blue Boy and Little Red with us. When they saw the lodge, they raised their noses and commenced to whine. It was not a good sign. Granpa went in first; he had to stoop to go through the door. I followed him.

There was only one room in the lodge. Willow John

lay on a bed of deer hides spread over spring boughs. He was naked. The long copper frame was withered like an old tree and one hand lay limp on the dirt floor.

Granpa whispered, "Willow John!"

Willow John opened his eyes. His eyes was faraway, but he grinned. "I knew you would come," he said, "and so, I waited." Granpa found a iron pot and sent me for water. I found it, trickling from rocks behind the lodge.

There was a fire pit just inside the door and Granpa built a fire and put the pot over it. He dropped strips of deer meat in the water; and after they had boiled, raised Willow John's head in the cradle of his arm and spooned the broth down him.

I got blankets from a corner and we covered Willow John. He didn't open his eyes. Night come on. Me and Granpa kept the fire going in the fire pit. The wind whistled on the mountaintop and whined around the corners of the lodge.

Granpa set cross-legged before the fire and the light flickered over his face, changing it from old, to older . . . making it look like rock crags and clefts in the shadows of his cheekbones until all I could see was the eyes looking at the fire; burning black, not like flames, but like embers going out. I curled around the fire pit and slept.

It was morning when I woke. The fire was beating back fog drifting in the door. Granpa still set by the fire; like he hadn't moved atall, though I know he had kept it burning.

Willow John stirred. Me and Granpa went to his side, and his eyes was open. He raised his hand and pointed. "Take me outside."

"It's cold out," Granpa said.

"I know," Willow John whispered.

Granpa had a hard time getting Willow John into his arms, for he was total limp. I tried to help.

Granpa carried him out the door and I dragged the

spring boughs behind them. Granpa clambered up the bank
of the fold to a high point and we laid Willow John on the
spring boughs. We wrapped him in blankets and put his
boot moccasins on his feet. Granpa folded hides and
propped up his head.

The sun broke through behind us and chased the fog
into the deeps, searching shade. Willow John was looking
west, across the wild mountains and deep hollows, as far
as you could see; toward the Nations.

Granpa went to the lodge and come back with Willow
John's long knife. He put it in his hand. Willow John
raised the knife and pointed to an old fir-pine that was
bent and twisted. He said, "When I have gone, put the
body there, close to her. She has dropped many young and
warmed me and sheltered me. It will be good. The food
will give her two more seasons."

"We will," Granpa said.

"Tell Bee," Willow John whispered, "it will be better
next time."

"I will," Granpa said.

He set down by Willow John and taken his hand. I set
on the other side and taken his other hand.

"I will wait for you," Willow John told Granpa.

"We will come," Granpa said.

I told Willow John that more than likely, it was the
flu; Granma had said that it was going around practical
everywheres. I told him I was might near certain that
we could get him on his feet and down the mountain
where he could stay with us. I told him the whole thing
was to get on his feet, and then he could more than likely
make it.

He grinned at me and squeezed my hand. "You have
good heart, Little Tree; but I do not want to stay. I want
to go. I will wait for you."

I cried. I told Willow John reckin if he couldn't figger
on staying a little longer, maybe he could go next year

when it would be warmer. I told him the hickor'nut crop would be good this winter. I told him you could might near see right off that the deer would be fat.

He grinned, but he didn't answer me.

He looked far out over the mountains, toward the west; like me and Granpa was not there anymore. He begun his passing song, telling the spirits he was coming. The death song.

It begun low in his throat and rose higher and commenced to get thinner.

In a little while you couldn't tell if it was the wind, or Willow John that you heard. His eyes got dimmer as his throat muscles moved weaker.

Me and Granpa saw the spirit slipping away farther back in his eyes and we felt it leaving his body. Then he was gone.

The wind whooshed across us and bent the old fir-pine. Granpa said it was Willow John, and he had a strong spirit. We watched it, bending just the tops of the trees on the ridges, moving down the side of the mountain and raising a flock of crows into the air. They cawed and cawed and set off down the mountain with Willow John.

Me and Granpa set and watched him move out of sight over the rims and humps of the mountains. We set a long time.

Granpa said Willow John would be back, and that we would feel him in the wind and hear him on the talking fingers of the trees. Which we would.

Me and Granpa taken our long knives and dug the hole; as close to the old fir-pine as we could get it. We dug it deep. Granpa wrapped another blanket around Willow John's body and we laid it in the hole. He put Willow John's hat in the hole too, and let the long knife stay in his hand; where he gripped it tight.

We piled rocks heavy and deep over the body of Willow John. Granpa said the 'coons must be kept away, for Willow John was determined the tree was to have the food.

The sun was setting in the west when I follered Granpa down from the mountaintop. We had left the lodge as we had found it. Granpa carried a deer shirt of Willow John's to give to Granma.

When we reached the hollow, it was after midnight. I heard a mourning dove far back, calling. It was not answered. I knew it called for Willow John.

Granma lit the lamp when we come in. Granpa laid Willow John's shirt on the table and did not say anything. Granma knew.

We didn't go to church after that. I didn't care, for Willow John would not be there.

We was to have two more years together; me and Granpa and Granma. Maybe we knew time was getting close, but we didn't speak of it. Granma went everywhere now with me and Granpa. We lived it full. We pointed out things like the reddest of the leaves in the fall, to make sure the others saw it, the bluest violet in the spring, so we all tasted and shared the feeling together.

Granpa's step got slower. His moccasins dragged some when he walked. I toted more of the fruit jar wares in my tow sack and taken to handling more of the heavy work. We didn't mention it.

Granpa showed me how to curve the down swing of an axe, so you moved through a log fast and easy. I pulled more of the corn than he did, leaving the ears easiest to reach for him; but I didn't say anything. I remembered what Granpa had said about ol' Ringer feeling he was still of worth. That last fall, ol' Sam died.

I told Granpa reckin we hadn't better see about another mule, and Granpa said it was a long time 'til spring; let's wait and see.

We taken the high trail more regular; me and Granpa and Granma. The climb was slower for them, but they loved to set and watch the mountain rims.

It was on the high trail that Granpa slipped and fell. He

didn't get up. Me and Granma sided him down the mountain and he kept saying, "I'll be all right d'rectly." But he wasn't. We put him abed.

Pine Billy come by. He stayed with us and set up with Granpa. Granpa wanted to hear his fiddle and Pine Billy played. There in the lamplight, with his homemade haircropping hanging over his ears, and his long neck bent over the fiddle, Pine Billy played. Tears run down his face onto the fiddle and dropped on his overalls.

Granpa said, "Quit crying, Pine Billy. Ye're messing up the music. I want to hear the fiddle."

Pine Billy choked and said, "I ain't crying. I cotched a c-c-cold." Then he dropped his fiddle and flung hisself at the foot of Granpa's bed and laid his head in the bedclothes. He heaved and cried. Pine Billy never was one to hold hisself in about anything.

Granpa raised up his head and hollered—weak, "Ye damn idjit; ye're gittin' Red Eagle snuff all over the bed sheets!" Which he was.

I cried too, but I didn't let Granpa see me.

Granpa's body mind commenced to stumble and sleep. His spirit mind taken over. He talked to Willow John a lot. Granma held his head in her arms and whispered in his ear.

Granpa come back to his body mind. He wanted his hat, which I got; and he put it on his head. I held his hand and he grinned. "It was good, Little Tree. Next time, it will be better. I'll be seein' ye." And he slipped off; like Willow John had done.

I knew it was going to happen, but I didn't believe it. Granma laid on the bed by Granpa, holding him tight. Pine Billy was bawling on the foot of the bed.

I slipped out of the cabin. The hounds was baying and whining, for they knew. I walked down the hollow trail and taken the cutoff trail. I was not follering Granpa, and then I knew the world had come to an end.

I was blinded and fell and got up and walked and fell

again; I don't know how many times. I come to the crossroads store and I told Mr. Jenkins. Granpa was dead.

Mr. Jenkins was too old to walk and he sent his son, a full-growed man, to go back with me. He led me by the hand, like I was might near a baby, for I could not see the trail, nor know where I was going.

Mr. Jenkins' son and Pine Billy made the box. I tried to help. I recollected Granpa said you was obligated to pitch in when folks was trying to do for you; but I wasn't much account at it. Pine Billy cried so much, he wasn't neither. He hit his thumb with the hammer.

They carried Granpa up the high trail. Granma leading, and Pine Billy and Mr. Jenkins' son carrying the box. Me and the hounds come behind. Pine Billy kept crying, which made it hard on me to hold myself in, not wanting to trouble Granma. The hounds whined.

I knew where Granma was taking Granpa. It was to his secret place; high on the mountain trail where he watched the day birth and never got tired of it and never quit saying, "She's coming alive!" like each time was the first time he had ever seen it. Maybe it was. Maybe every birthing is different and Granpa could see that it was and knew.

It was the place Granpa had taken me first, and so I knew Granpa kinned me.

Granma didn't look as we lowered Granpa in the ground. She watched the mountains, faroff, and she didn't cry.

The wind was strong, there on the mountaintop and it lifted her hair-braids and streamed them out behind her. Pine Billy and Mr. Jenkins' son walked off, back down the trail. Me and the hounds watched Granma awhile, then we slipped away.

We waited, setting under a tree halfway down the trail, for Granma to come. It was dusk when she did.

I tried to pick up Granpa's load and mine too. I ran the still, but I know our wares was not as good.

Granma got out all Mr. Wine's figgering books and

pushed me on learning. I went to the settlement alone and brought back other books. I read them now, by the fireplace, while Granma listened and watched the fire. She said I done good.

Ol' Rippitt died, and later that winter, ol' Maud.

It was just before spring. I come from the Narrows down the hollow trail. I saw Granma setting on the back porch. She had moved her rocker there.

She didn't watch me as I come down the hollow. She was looking up, toward the high trail. I knew she was gone.

She had put on the orange and green and red and gold dress that Granpa loved. She had printed out a note and pinned it on her bosom. It said:

Little Tree, I must go. Like you feel the trees, feel for us when you are listening. We will wait for you. Next time will be better. All is well. Granma.

I carried the tiny body into the cabin and put it on the bed and set with her through the day. Blue Boy and Little Red set too.

That evening I went and found Pine Billy. Pine Billy set up the night with me and Granma. He cried and played his fiddle. He played the wind . . . and the Dog Star . . . and the mountain rims . . . and the day birthing . . . and dying. Me and Pine Billy knew Granma and Granpa was listening.

We made the box next morning and carried her up the high trail and laid her beside Granpa. I taken the old marriage stick and buried the ends in piles of stone me and Pine Billy put at the head of each grave.

I seen the notches they made for me; right down near the end of the stick. They was deep and happy notches.

I lasted out the winter; me and Blue Boy and Little Red, until spring. Then I went to Hangin' Gap and buried the still's copper pot and worm. I was not much good at it, and had not learned the trade as I had ought to. I knew Granpa would not want anybody else using it to turn out bad wares.

I took the whiskey trade money that Granma had set out for me and determined I would head west, across the mountains to the Nations. Blue Boy and Little Red went with me. We just closed the cabin door one morning and walked away.

At the farms I asked for work, if they would not let me keep Blue Boy and Little Red then I would move on. Granpa said a feller owed that much to his hounds. Which is right.

Little Red fell through creek ice in the Arkansas Ozarks and died like a hound ought to die, in the mountains. Me and Blue Boy made it to the Nations, where there was no Nation.

We worked on the farms, going west, and then the ranches on the flats.

One evening late, Blue Boy come aside my horse. He laid down and couldn't get up. He couldn't go anymore. I taken him up, acrost my saddle, and we turned our backs on the red settin' sun of the Cimarron. We headed east.

I would not get my job back, riding off this way, but I didn't care. I had bought the horse and saddle for fifteen dollars and they was mine.

Me and Blue Boy was huntin' us a mountain.

Before day we found one. It wasn't much of a mountain, more like a hill, but Blue Boy whimpered when he seen it. I toted him to the top as the sun broke the east. I dug him a grave and he laid and watched.

He couldn't raise his head, but he let me know he knew it; for he stiffened a ear and kept his eyes on me. After that, I held Blue Boy's head, settin' on the ground. He licked my hand, when he could.

In a little while he passed on, easy, and dropped his

head over my arm. I buried him deep and rocked his grave heavy against the creatures.

With his nose sense, I figgered more than likely Blue Boy was already halfway to the mountains.

He'd have no trouble atall catching up with Granpa.